CY YOUNG AWARD
WINNERS

CY YOUNG
AWARD WINNERS

KEN YOUNG

WALKER AND COMPANY · NEW YORK

First published in the United States of America in 1994 by Walker
Publishing Company, Inc.

Published simultaneously in Canada by Thomas Allen & Son Canada,
Limited, Markham, Ontario

Library of Congress Cataloging-in-Publication Data
Young, Ken.
Cy Young award winners / Ken Young.
p.   cm.
Includes index.
ISBN 0-8027-8300-7. —ISBN 0-8027-8301-5
1. Pitchers (Baseball)—United States—Biography.   2. Cy Young
Award.   I. Title.
GV865.A1Y68   1994
796.357'092'2 —dc20
[B]   93-40418
CIP

Book design by Ron Monteleone

Printed in the United States of America

2 4 6 8 10 9 7 5 3 1

CONTENTS

ACKNOWLEDGMENTS

A number of people helped me with this project, and I would like to thank them here. They include: David Fischer, Stephanie Krasnow, Linda Verigan, and John Walters at *Sports Illustrated*; the *Sports Illustrated* Library; my nephews, Mike Kurtz and Matt Barker, who provided me with research assistance; the many public relations officials at major league teams; all the former and current players who agreed to be interviewed; and Emily Easton, my editor.

I must also thank my daughter, Emily, who helped me keep my sense of humor and perspective. Most of all, I would like to thank my wife, Debby, for her constant encouragement, editorial suggestions, and understanding.

INTRODUCTION

At the end of each baseball season, the American League and the National League honor their best pitcher with the Cy Young Award. The award is named for Denton True "Cy" Young, who—in a twenty-two-year pitching career that lasted from 1890 to 1911—won more games (511) than any player in the history of the sport.

Young was a right-hander with a tremendous fastball. He was given his nickname early in his career by a catcher who was warming him up one day. Several of Young's hard throws eluded the catcher, each time smashing into the backstop. When the catcher finally took a good look at the backstop, he saw that a number of the boards had been broken by Young's throws. "Gee, it looks like a cyclone hit it," said the catcher. Cy Young had arrived.

Young pitched until he was forty-four years old, and his 511 career wins far outdistance runner-up Walter Johnson's 416. He pitched three no-hitters and is also the all-time leader in complete games and innings pitched. Young was elected to the Baseball Hall of Fame in 1937.

The first Cy Young Award was presented in 1956 to Don Newcombe of the Brooklyn Dodgers for his 27–7 record. At the time, the award honored the best pitcher in *all* of baseball. Beginning in 1967, though, the award was given to the best pitcher in each *league*.

This book includes profiles of ten players whose outstanding seasons earned them baseball's highest honor for pitchers. Although space prevents me from including profiles of all the Cy Young Award winners, I must mention a few who are not included in this book. Warren Spahn, the 1957 winner for the Milwaukee Braves, won 363 games in his career, the most by a left-hander. The Chicago White Sox's Early Wynn is the oldest winner; he was thirty-nine when he was named the 1959 Cy Young winner. Gaylord Perry won in 1972 with the Cleveland Indians and in 1978 with the San Diego Padres, the only person to have won the award in both leagues. In 1974, the Los Angeles Dodgers' Mike Marshall became the first relief pitcher to be honored.

There are also many outstanding pitchers who, for one reason or another, never won a Cy Young Award. Nolan Ryan, for example, has struck out more batters than anyone in baseball history and has pitched an all-time-best seven no-hitters. He never won the Cy Young Award, though, so you won't find him profiled here.

What you will find here are the stories of some pitchers who had amazing seasons — and careers. These are the people who make baseball so much fun to watch, year after year.

Play ball!

1. WHITEY FORD

THE CHAIRMAN OF THE BOARD

No one has ever pitched more consecutive scoreless innings in World Series history than Whitey Ford, the New York Yankee left-hander. And it is unlikely that his record will ever be broken.

Ford began his scoreless-innings streak in the 1960 World Series, against the Pittsburgh Pirates. He threw two shutouts against Pittsburgh, giving him 18 scoreless innings.

The Yankees returned to the World Series in 1961, this time facing the Cincinnati Reds. Ford shut out the Reds in his first game, giving him 27 consecutive scoreless innings.

In his second game against the Reds, Ford threw five more scoreless innings before leaving the game with a freak injury to his foot, the result of fouling two consecutive pitches off his toe. It was during this game that Ford broke the previous World Series record of 29⅔ consecutive scoreless innings pitched.

That record had been set by Babe Ruth, who was an excellent pitcher before becoming known for his home runs.

In the 1962 World Series, Ford pitched a scoreless first inning against the San Francisco Giants. Finally, in the second inning, the Giants scored a run. Ford had pitched a total of 33⅔ scoreless innings, a World Series record many think will last forever.

Edward Charles Ford was born on October 21, 1928, in New York City. Nicknamed "Whitey" because of his light blond hair, Ford played first base throughout high school.

In the spring of 1946, he went to a Yankee tryout. Despite his best efforts, the Yankees were unimpressed.

"They didn't think too much of me, at least as a first baseman," said Ford. "But then one scout came up to me and said, 'Did you ever think about pitching?'

"The next thing I knew, they had me throwing with a catcher. Someone taught me how to throw a curve, and I began to think of myself as a pitcher."

Ford pitched all summer in a Long Island league and was a natural. His team played 36 games, with Ford pitching—and winning—18 of those. Despite having been a pitcher for such a short time, he attracted the attention of several teams. At the end of the summer, the Yankees, the Brooklyn Dodgers, and the Boston Red Sox were all interested in this rising star. The Yankees got him, though, by offering him a $7,000 signing bonus.

The eighteen-year-old Ford began his professional career in the Yankee minor leagues at Butler (Pennsylvania). Although he rarely looked brilliant, he usually managed to win. He finished his first professional season with an impressive 13–4 record.

Ford continued to be a winner as he marched steadily through the Yankees' minor league system. He went 16–8 the next year with Norfolk (Virginia) in the Piedmont League, and followed that with a 16–5 year at Binghamton (New York) in the Eastern League.

He began the 1950 season with Kansas City in the American Association, the highest level of minor league competition. His record was 6–3 when the Yankees decided he was ready for the big time.

The Yankees were in the middle of a pennant race with the Detroit Tigers and the Boston Red Sox, but the pressure had no effect on Ford. The confident, outgoing left-hander quickly showed American League batters that he was ready for the major leagues, setting an American League record of nine consecutive wins at the start of a career.

Ford finished the season with a 9–1 record, and his outstanding pitching helped propel the Yankees into the World Series. He gave baseball fans a taste of what he was to accomplish in the future when, in his first Series appearance, he did not give up a single earned run against the Philadelphia Phillies.

At the end of the World Series, Ford was drafted into the Army, where he spent the next two years. He returned in 1953 and continued his baseball career, finishing the year with an 18–6 record.

Ford was quickly becoming the ace of the Yankees. He won 16 games for them in 1954, and another 18 in 1955. In September of 1955, he tied a major league record by pitching two consecutive one-hitters.

Ford was such a good pitcher that it was unusual when he lost. Year after year, his winning percentage was among the best in all of baseball. Ford was not that big (5'10", 180 pounds) and did not possess an overpowering fastball. But he had great breaking pitches that, combined with his extraordinary control, continually frustrated the game's best hitters.

In 1956, Ford won 19 games while losing only 6. His 2.47 ERA led the American League. For all his brilliance, though, he had yet to win 20 games, the traditional standard of pitching excellence.

Outfielder Mickey Mantle was Ford's closest friend. Mantle and Ford had single rooms on the road, the only Yankees without roommates. The two friends usually got adjoining rooms and frequently kept the door open between their two suites.

Infielder Billy Martin, who would later become a Yankee manager, was a good friend of both Ford and

Used by permission of the National Baseball Library, Cooperstown, New York

Mantle. The three teammates were well-known for their postgame parties. Their most memorable off-the-field incident occurred in 1957. Ford, Mantle, and several of their teammates had gone to the Copacabana, a famous New York City nightclub, to celebrate Martin's twenty-ninth birthday.

A fight broke out at the club, and Ford and the others were fined. Martin received the toughest punishment: He was traded to the Kansas City Athletics.

A week later, Ford was pitching against the Athletics. He had a big lead, and Martin was at bat. Ford fooled his friend and former teammate with a curve, then smiled and said, "Same thing," telling Martin what pitch was coming.

Ford expected Martin to hit a single or a double, but Martin jumped on the curve and hit a home run. Martin celebrated so much as he rounded the bases that Ford momentarily regretted helping his old friend.

Ford possessed incredible confidence on the mound. He was clearly the leader on the field and gave his teammates the feeling that they were unbeatable when he was pitching.

Ford had a reputation as a clutch pitcher. If you needed to win a single game, the theory went, you wanted Ford as your pitcher.

Ford's teammates knew and appreciated the value of their star pitcher. They realized that he helped make all of them better. They nicknamed Ford "The

Chairman of the Board," because they knew he controlled their destiny.

Off the field, Ford was a leader in the clubhouse. He went out of his way to speak with and encourage the younger players and those who were not stars.

He was also known as the team comic. He was quick to laugh and was well-known for his practical jokes, which served an important role by keeping his teammates relaxed.

Ford carried this fun-loving attitude onto the playing field. Players throughout the league suspected Ford used a spitball and other illegal pitches. According to Yankee shortstop Tony Kubek, Ford didn't need the spitball to get batters out. He used the illegal pitch for the sheer fun of fooling the batters.

While Ford was confident on the field, he was very humble off of it. His inability to reach the 20-win plateau for so long did not bother him. He cared only about the Yankees' winning the pennant.

The same philosophy applied to strikeouts and complete games. Ford was content to let batters hit the ball to one of his teammates. In the later innings of games, he willingly gave the ball to Luis Arroyo and other relievers.

In 1960, the Yankees faced the Pittsburgh Pirates in the World Series. The Series opened in Pittsburgh, and manager Casey Stengel decided to save Ford for Game 3 in Yankee Stadium, where Ford was practically unbeatable.

Ford was surprised that he didn't start the opener, and his teammates were angry. How could you have the best big-game pitcher in baseball and not use him as often as possible?

Ford pitched a shutout in Game 3 and followed with yet another one in Game 6, tying the Series at three games each. But because pitching consecutive games is too difficult, he could only watch as the Yankees lost Game 7. Afterward, a visibly upset Mantle stated that Stengel's decision not to use Ford in Game 1 (which would have made Ford available to pitch Game 4 and Game 7) had cost the Yankees the Series.

For all his talent, Ford had still not won 20 games in a season. Strangely enough, it was Ford's outstanding ability that was preventing him from accomplishing the feat. Ford was so good that manager Casey Stengel used him only in big games, against the toughest opponents. Ford was frequently matched against the opponent's top pitcher, making his impressive win-loss record even more remarkable.

"One game wasn't more important to me than any other," said Ford, offering an explanation of why he did so well in the big games. "I didn't approach a World Series game any differently than I did a regular season game."

In 1961, Ralph Houk took over as the Yankee manager. Houk had watched Ford pitch and, unlike

USED BY PERMISSION OF THE NATIONAL BASEBALL LIBRARY, COOPERSTOWN, NEW YORK

Stengel, was determined to use him as frequently as possible.

Ford was thrilled when he heard the news. "I wanted to pitch in as many games as possible," said Ford. "Houk's decision meant I would get a lot more work."

That year Ford started more games (a league high 39) than he ever had, and he also led the league in innings pitched (283). The result was one of the greatest years a pitcher ever had.

The season got off to a slow start, with Ford and the Yankees losing the opener to the Minnesota Twins, 6–0. But Ford won his next six starts before losing to Boston, 2–1, at the end of May.

Ford practically *owned* the American League in June. He started and won eight games that month, something no other pitcher in the league had ever done.

Ford finished the year with 25 wins. Remarkable for anyone but Ford, he lost only 4. At one point he won 14 consecutive games. When it came time to name the Cy Young Award winner, Ford was the obvious choice.

"I wasn't surprised," said Ford. "I knew I had been the best in the American League that year, so I figured I had a good chance."

Ford benefited from playing on some of the strongest teams in baseball history. His teammates included Mantle, Roger Maris, Yogi Berra, Elston

Howard, Tony Kubek, and Bobby Richardson. Some say this gave Ford a double advantage. Not only did he benefit from the support of his talented teammates, he also avoided having to pitch to them!

Ford's teammates gave him plenty of runs, but they also provided him with a solid defense. "Defense is important to me," said Ford. "I'm a ground-ball pitcher, and I need teammates who can make the plays." In third baseman Clete Boyer, shortstop Kubek and second baseman Richardson, Ford was given as good a defense as any pitcher could ask for.

Thirty-five-year-old reliever Luis Arroyo was a key factor in Ford's Cy Young Award season. Arroyo had been only an average pitcher for most of his major league career, but in 1961 he became an outstanding one. He finished the year with a 15–5 record and 29 saves. Ford won 25 games that year, and Arroyo saved 15 of those.

Despite Ford's incredible year as a pitcher in 1961, most of the attention was focused on one of the game's most impressive home run records: Babe Ruth's 60 home runs in a single season. Not one, but two Yankees—Mickey Mantle and Roger Maris— were chasing Ruth.

Reporters surrounded the two players constantly, making it difficult for them to focus on their playing. Although Mantle faded late in the year due to injuries, Maris finally broke Ruth's record by hitting 61 home runs.

"Roger showed a lot of courage that year," said Ford. "I thought it was amazing the way he performed while still handling the pressure of breaking Ruth's record."

Ford followed his Cy Young year with a 17–8 season in 1962. He almost matched his 1961 year in 1963, finishing the season with a 24–7 record.

In most years, a record like that would have guaranteed Ford another Cy Young Award. But in the National League, Sandy Koufax was completing a 25–5 season for the Los Angeles Dodgers, a performance that would earn him National League MVP honors. The 1963 Cy Young Award belonged to Koufax.

Ford and Koufax squared off against each other in game one of the 1963 World Series. The Yankees were heavy favorites, but the Dodgers didn't listen to the oddsmakers. Behind Koufax's Series-record 15 strikeouts, Los Angeles took Game 1 and went on to sweep the Yankees, four games to none.

Ford pitched in 11 World Series for the Yankees. He was 2–0 in three of them (1955, '60, and '61), and is baseball's all-time leader in World Series games won (10) and lost (8).

"I'm not much for records or individual accomplishments," said Ford. "But pitching in eleven World Series is something special. To me, that's what I'm proudest of."

Ford had shoulder problems late in his career. Finally, in 1967, the pain and frustration became too much, and he retired. Along with the departure of Mickey Mantle in 1968, Ford's retirement symbolized the end of the Yankee dynasty.

Ford left baseball as the game's winningest pitcher. His 236–106 record gave him a winning percentage of .690, tops for players with a minimum of 200 decisions.

His career World Series records also include 94 strikeouts. His numerous Yankee records include career shutouts (45), shutouts in a season (8), career strikeouts (1,956), strikeouts in a single game (15), and consecutive wins (14).

"Ford threw that slider away from you and just dared you to hit it," said former Detroit Tigers star Jim Northrup. "He was a master."

WHITEY FORD—CAREER STATISTICS

YEAR	CLUB	LEAGUE	G	IP	W	L	H	R	ER	SO	BB	ERA
1947	BUTLER	MID. ATL.	24	157	13	4	151	86	67	114	58	3.84
1948	NORFOLK	PIEDMONT	30	216	16	8	182	83	62	171	113	2.58
1949	BINGHAMTON	EASTERN	26	168	16	5	118	38	30	151	54	1.61
1950	KANSAS CITY	AMER. ASSOC.	12	95	6	3	81	39	34	80	48	3.22
1950	NEW YORK	AMERICAN	20	112	9	1	87	39	35	59	52	2.81
1951–52	NEW YORK	AMERICAN					(IN MILITARY SERVICE)					
1953	NEW YORK	AMERICAN	32	207	18	6	187	77	69	110	110	3.00
1954	NEW YORK	AMERICAN	34	211	16	8	170	72	66	125	101	2.82
1955	NEW YORK	AMERICAN	39	254	18	7	188	83	74	137	113	2.62
1956	NEW YORK	AMERICAN	31	226	19	6	187	70	62	141	84	2.47

Year	City	League										ERA
1957	NEW YORK	AMERICAN	24	129	11	5	114	46	37	84	53	2.58
1958	NEW YORK	AMERICAN	30	219	14	7	174	62	49	145	62	2.01
1959	NEW YORK	AMERICAN	35	204	16	10	194	82	69	114	89	3.04
1960	NEW YORK	AMERICAN	33	193	12	9	168	76	66	85	65	3.08
1961	NEW YORK	AMERICAN	39	283	25	4	242	108	101	209	92	3.21
1962	NEW YORK	AMERICAN	38	258	17	8	243	90	83	160	69	2.90
1963	NEW YORK	AMERICAN	38	269	24	7	240	94	82	189	56	2.74
1964	NEW YORK	AMERICAN	39	245	17	6	212	67	58	172	57	2.13
1965	NEW YORK	AMERICAN	37	244	16	13	241	97	88	162	50	3.25
1966	NEW YORK	AMERICAN	22	73	2	5	79	33	20	43	24	2.47
1967	NEW YORK	AMERICAN	7	44	2	4	40	11	8	21	9	1.64
MAJOR LEAGUE TOTALS			498	3171	236	106	2766	1107	967	1956	1086	2.74

2. SANDY KOUFAX

Amputation.

That's what Los Angeles Dodger pitcher Sandy Koufax, frustrated and depressed for most of the 1962 season by the blisters on his left index finger, feared might have to happen.

Koufax's record that year was 14–7, a disappointment when compared to his 18–13 record the previous year when he was injury-free. The highlight had been his first no-hitter, against the newly created New York Mets, in which he had struck out the side in the first inning on only nine pitches. As the season ended, though, Koufax wondered if his injured finger would ever heal.

Whatever doubts he might have had were quickly erased in 1963. Eleven teams were shut out by Koufax, who threw his second career no-hitter (against the San Francisco Giants) en route to a 25–5 record. As a result of his brilliant season, he won both the Cy Young Award and the MVP Award.

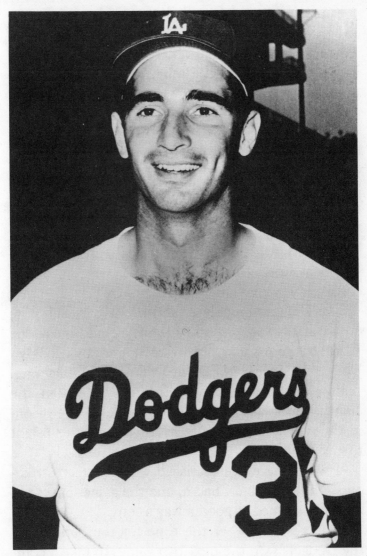

Koufax's efforts propelled the Dodgers into the 1963 World Series, where they faced the New York Yankees. Most impartial observers gave the Dodgers little chance against the mighty Yankees, who featured sluggers like Mickey Mantle and Roger Maris, and pitchers like Whitey Ford.

"I thought we'd have a tough fight," said Dodgers catcher Johnny Roseboro. "Boy, was I wrong."

Koufax, as expected, was the Dodgers' starting pitcher for Game 1. In the first inning, he struck out the first three Yankee batters—Tony Kubek, Bobby Richardson, and Tom Tresh. In the second inning, Mickey Mantle and Roger Maris went down on strikes as Koufax tied a World Series record of five consecutive strikeouts.

The Dodgers quickly established a big lead. The only question was whether Koufax could break the World Series record of 14 strikeouts, set by Brooklyn Dodgers pitcher Carl Erskine against the Yankees ten years earlier. Koufax tied Erskine's record in the eighth inning with two strikeouts. He set the record in the ninth, dramatically striking out Harry Bright to end the game.

"I would have been satisfied with fourteen strikeouts," he said, "but I had to end the game some way, and that seemed as good a way as any."

Koufax's victory set the tone for the Series, and the Dodgers won the next two games to take a commanding three-games-to-none lead. As Koufax prepared to pitch Game Four, a *New York Daily News* headline shouted, THREE IN A ROW—NOW KOUFAX!

Koufax and the Dodgers won Game 4 to sweep the Series, becoming the first team in history to sweep the Yankees in the World Series. Koufax had 8 strikeouts in the final game, and his 23 for the Series set another record.

Sanford Braun was born in Brooklyn in 1935. His parents divorced when he was three. When his mother remarried, Sandy took the last name of his new father, Irving Koufax.

Koufax's athletic talent was apparent at an early age, even in nontraditional "sports" like snowball throwing. Koufax threw his snowballs harder and farther than any of his friends.

Koufax was a lefty and, like many left-handers, he played first base. One day, while playing for Brooklyn's Lafayette High School, he made the long throw to third base. The hard and accurate throw so impressed Koufax's coach, Milton Laurie, that he decided to make Koufax a pitcher.

Although he enjoyed baseball, basketball was Koufax's favorite sport. He won a basketball scholarship to the University of Cincinnati, where he was the leading rebounder and averaged 9.7 points per game for the Bearcat freshman team.

Following basketball season, Koufax approached the baseball coach and offered to pitch. In 31 innings of pitching, Koufax's record was 3–1. More noticeable were his 51 strikeouts, an average of more than 1.5 an inning.

Koufax's potential did not escape the Brooklyn Dodger scout who saw him pitch. Even Koufax's lack of pitching experience could not hide the fact that he possessed a remarkable fastball. The scout offered Koufax a signing bonus of $20,000—not particularly large for that time—and Koufax became a Dodger.

At the time Koufax signed, baseball had a rule that a club that paid a player a signing bonus of $10,000 or more must keep the "bonus baby" on its major league roster for at least two years. This was to prevent the wealthier clubs from signing all the best talent and then hiding them in their minor league system. For Koufax, the rule meant that he would get his education sitting on the Dodger bench, when what he needed was actual game experience as a pitcher.

Koufax had an arm other players only dreamed about, but he was wild and inexperienced. By the end of his second year, in 1956, he had pitched only about 100 innings of major league baseball and was walking almost as many batters as he struck out.

"In the early days, he never threw the ball over the plate," said Roseboro. "He threw hard, but you never knew where the ball was going to go."

In 1957, Koufax began to show promise. He appeared in 34 games, posting a 5–4 record and striking out 122 batters. An 11–11 season the following year—when the Dodgers moved to Los Angeles—was followed by an 8–6 record in 1959. He tied Bob Feller's major league single-game record that year with 18 strikeouts against the San Francisco Giants, striking out the side in the ninth inning on only ten pitches. Koufax struck out 197 batters in 1960, but his record was a disappointing 8–13.

Koufax had been a major league pitcher for six years. His win-loss record was a very mediocre 36–40. He was so frustrated that he briefly considered quitting the game.

"Maybe the problem was that I never had a burning ambition to be a baseball player," said Koufax. "If I had, I might have realized sooner just how much work was involved."

Everyone agreed that Koufax had a strong arm, perhaps even a gifted one. The question was, could he control it? When Koufax pitched, the ball could go anywhere—over the plate or over the batter's head. If Koufax could learn to control his pitches, he had a chance to be a star.

And if he couldn't learn to control his pitches? Well, then he would end up as just another mediocre major league pitcher.

The Dodgers were patient with Koufax because they believed he could be special. Their suspicion was confirmed every time they discussed trades with other teams. Koufax was the one player everyone wanted.

"The Dodgers were getting ready to send him to the minors to work on his control," said Roseboro. "But he suddenly found that control—I'm not sure how or why it happened—and he went from being ordinary to exceptional. Everyone was shocked."

Here's how it happened. At spring training in 1961, catcher Norm Sherry told Koufax to stop trying to throw the ball so hard. Control, Sherry advised, was the key. With a combination of control and his sweeping curveball, Sherry continued, Koufax could become a successful pitcher.

Koufax took Sherry's advice and worked even harder to improve his control. The hard work paid off. Koufax quickly became one of the league's best pitchers, compiling an 18–13 record and striking out 269 batters.

After years of struggling to find the plate, control became one of Koufax's greatest strengths. He pitched 311 innings in 1963 and walked only 58 batters.

"Catching him became the easiest job in the world," said Johnny Roseboro. "The ball always came right to me. I never had to move.

"Hitters had what I call a 'comfortable' oh-for-four against Koufax," Roseboro continued. "They never had to worry about being knocked down, because his control was so good. But they still couldn't get their bat on the ball."

Koufax's 1964 season looked like it might be a repeat of his 1963 Cy Young and MVP year. He continued to dominate National League batters and pitched his third no-hitter in as many years. The no-hitter, which came against the Philadelphia Phillies, was nearly a perfect game. Koufax allowed only one base runner, Richie Allen, who walked on a 3–2 pitch.

On August 20, he improved his record to 19–5 with a 3–0 shutout and 13 strikeouts against the St. Louis Cardinals. While sliding into second base, though, Koufax landed hard on his left elbow. Although he finished the game, the injury was much more serious than it first appeared. Koufax's 1964 season was over and his career was threatened.

"The next morning I had to drag my arm out of bed like a log," said Koufax. "For an elbow, I had a knee. That's how thick it was."

Following a series of tests, it was determined that Koufax had arthritis, brought on by the wear and tear of pitching. The condition was not only irreversible, it would worsen.

To compensate, Koufax began pitching *only* in games, giving up his usual routine of throwing between starts. After pitching, he would place his arthritic elbow in a bucket of ice water to reduce any swelling. Although Koufax had no pain while pitching, he suffered after the games. Sometimes the pain was so bad that it was difficult for him to sleep.

Despite the increasing problems with his arm, Koufax was overpowering in 1965. He won 26 games while losing only 8, and his 382 strikeouts are still the record for a National League pitcher.

Koufax considered his strikeout record his greatest feat, ahead of even his perfect game. "A pitcher can get hot for one game and throw a no-hitter or strike out eighteen," he said. "But a season's succession of strikeouts shows a consistency that I think is important."

Koufax was a key participant that year in one of baseball's ugliest incidents. The Dodgers were playing their bitter rivals, the San Francisco Giants, and Koufax was pitching against Giants ace Juan Marichal.

"Marichal had knocked down a couple of our guys with some close pitches," said Roseboro, the Dodger catcher. "Usually your pitcher will retaliate by knocking down some of the other team's players. But Sandy didn't like to throw at people, so I decided I would take care of it."

The next time Marichal came to bat, several of Roseboro's return throws to Koufax came close to hitting Marichal. Roseboro and Marichal exchanged words, and then Marichal raised his bat with both hands and struck Roseboro in the head.

Koufax and players from both teams quickly subdued Marichal. Roseboro was hurt—he left the game with blood streaming down his face—but fortunately escaped permanent damage. Marichal was suspended for eight days and fined $1,750, a stiff punishment in those days.

Emotional outbursts were not part of Koufax's temperament. "I only saw Koufax get angry one time," said Roseboro. "He was pitching against the Cardinals, and Lou Brock stole second base, third base, and then scored.

"The next time he came up, Sandy hit him in the back and Brock crumbled to the ground in pain. I'm sure that's why Sandy never threw at hitters. He knew how much he could hurt them."

On September 9 of that year, Koufax pitched a perfect game—only the eighth in major league history—against the Chicago Cubs. He struck out 14 Cubs, including the last 6. His fourth career no-hitter made him the first pitcher to achieve that goal, breaking the record held by Bob Feller, Cy Young, and Larry Corcoran.

In the 1965 World Series, the Minnesota Twins quickly learned why Koufax was considered the best pitcher in baseball. "Sandy Koufax is the only pitcher I would pay to see warm up," said Minnesota manager Sam Mele before the start of the Series.

Mele saw more of Koufax than perhaps he would have liked. Koufax pitched two shutouts against the Twins, the second on only two days' rest, and led the

USED BY PERMISSION OF THE NATIONAL BASEBALL LIBRARY, COOPERSTOWN, NEW YORK

Dodgers to the world championship. Following the Series, Koufax was presented with his second Cy Young Award, an honor that surprised no one.

In 1966, Koufax and fellow Dodger pitcher Don Drysdale refused to report to spring training. They both thought they deserved to be paid larger salaries. Theirs was the first joint holdout, and they were the first to use an agent to negotiate their contracts.

Their holdout lasted 32 days, ending just before the season began. They didn't get as much money as they wanted, but they played an important role in baseball players' ongoing fight to be treated fairly by the owners.

The 1966 season was another great one for Koufax: a 27–9 record, his third Cy Young Award, and a pennant-clinching shutout over the Philadelphia Phillies in the final game of the season. Although the Dodgers lost the World Series to the Baltimore Orioles, Dodger fans looked forward to watching baseball's best pitcher in 1967.

Koufax had other ideas. He had grown weary of the pain in his arthritic elbow and feared he might permanently injure himself if he continued pitching. On November 18, at the age of thirty, he stunned the sports world by retiring.

Other great players had lingered past their time, tarnishing the memory of their greatness. Koufax chose to retire at the peak of his ability, guaranteeing that his greatness would never be forgotten.

Koufax finished his career with 165 wins and 87 losses, a winning percentage of .655. Only five other pitchers in baseball history have a better career winning percentage. Koufax's overall record is even more remarkable when you consider that for the first six years of his career it was 36–40.

From 1963 to 1966, Koufax *averaged* 24 wins, 307 strikeouts, and a 1.85 ERA. He won the Cy Young Award three times in four years, becoming the first player to win two and then the first to win three. All three Cy Youngs were unanimous; no other pitcher had ever won the award by a unanimous vote. From 1962 to 1966, he won a record five consecutive ERA titles. He even won a Most Valuable Player (MVP) Award, an honor rarely given to a pitcher.

It should also be noted that Koufax won his Cy Young Awards when only one award was given for all of baseball. It was not until 1967 that a Cy Young winner was selected for each league.

In 1972, Koufax became the youngest player ever voted into the Baseball Hall of Fame. Although his career was cut short by injury, there can be no doubt that he was truly *the* pitcher of the 1960s.

SANDY KOUFAX—CAREER STATISTICS

YEAR	CLUB	LEAGUE	G	IP	W	L	H	R	ER	SO	BB	ERA
1955	BROOKLYN	NATIONAL	12	42	2	2	33	15	14	30	28	3.00
1956	BROOKLYN	NATIONAL	16	59	2	4	66	37	32	30	29	4.88
1957	BROOKLYN	NATIONAL	34	104	5	4	83	49	45	122	51	3.89
1958	LOS ANGELES	NATIONAL	40	159	11	11	132	89	79	131	105	4.47
1959	LOS ANGELES	NATIONAL	35	153	8	6	136	74	69	173	92	4.06
1960	LOS ANGELES	NATIONAL	37	175	8	13	133	83	76	197	100	3.91
1961	LOS ANGELES	NATIONAL	42	256	18	13	212	117	100	269	96	3.52
1962	LOS ANGELES	NATIONAL	28	184	14	7	134	61	52	216	57	2.54
1963	LOS ANGELES	NATIONAL	40	311	25	5	214	68	65	306	58	1.88
1964	LOS ANGELES	NATIONAL	29	223	19	5	154	49	43	223	53	1.74
1965	LOS ANGELES	NATIONAL	43	336	26	8	216	90	76	382	71	2.04
1966	LOS ANGELES	NATIONAL	41	323	27	9	241	74	62	317	77	1.73
MAJOR LEAGUE TOTALS			397	2325	165	87	1754	806	713	2396	817	2.76

3. DENNY McLAIN

THE LAST 30-GAME WINNER

When Detroit Tiger pitcher Denny McLain took the mound on September 14, 1968, at Tiger Stadium, the whole country was watching. But they were not watching to see the Tigers or their opponent, the Oakland Athletics, grab another victory. Sports fans across the nation were watching to see history made.

McLain had already won 29 games that season. He was trying for the rarest of pitching accomplishments, more unusual than a no-hitter: the 30-win season.

Today we say a pitcher is great if he wins 25 games in a season. And with good reason. Pitching has changed dramatically in the last twenty-five years. Relief pitchers are used much more frequently now, and they get a lot of victories that used to go to the starting pitchers. Also, most teams now use five starting pitchers instead of four, meaning that there are fewer games for any one player to pitch.

But even in 1968, a 30-win season was almost un-heard of. There had only been *twelve* 30-game win-ners since 1900. Most of those had pitched in the first twenty years of the century.

Between 1920 and 1968, there were only two 30-game winners. Lefty Grove accomplished the feat in 1931, winning 31 games for the Philadelphia Ath-letics. Dizzy Dean did it in 1934, winning 30 games for the St. Louis Cardinals. It had been thirty-four years since someone had won 30 games.

Dean was among those present as McLain took the mound that September day. The fans could barely contain their excitement. McLain had been practi-cally unbeatable all season, and they were sure that he would accomplish his historic feat that day.

The A's took a 2–0 lead in the fourth inning when future Hall of Famer Reggie Jackson hit a home run with a man on base. The Tigers rallied to take the lead in the bottom of the inning, scoring three times.

The A's scored one run in the fifth, and the game remained tied until Reggie Jackson came to bat in the ninth inning. Jackson always had a flair for the dramatic and was at his best in critical situations. He hit his second home run of the game off McLain, giving the A's the lead and breaking the hearts of Tiger fans.

But the Tigers weren't finished yet. They had won

a lot of games in the last inning, so being behind didn't worry them.

"Come-from-behind wins were almost our trademark that year," said Bill Freehan, the Tigers' catcher. "We always scored a lot of runs when McLain pitched, and we believed we were going to win that game in the ninth inning."

Al Kaline, a Tiger legend and another future Hall of Famer, batted for McLain in the ninth inning. Kaline drew a walk, sparking a Tiger rally. With only one out, the Tigers had tied the score. Mickey Stanley, representing the winning run and the historic thirtieth victory for McLain, was on third.

Tiger slugger Willie Horton was the batter. The Oakland outfield was drawn in close to the infield, to try to prevent Stanley from scoring.

Tiger fans were standing, pleading with Horton to get the game-winning hit. McLain sat in the dugout, watching nervously with his teammates.

They didn't have to watch for long, as Horton hit a long fly ball to left field. The A's left fielder could only watch as the ball sailed far over his head for the game-winning hit.

McLain raced out of the dugout to hug Horton and Stanley. The other Tigers also charged onto the field, and lifted McLain onto their shoulders.

Photographers, television crews, and fans swarmed

COURTESY OF THE DETROIT TIGERS

around the cheering players. McLain had done it. He was a 30-game winner.

And there hasn't been another one since.

Dennis Dale McLain was born in Chicago on March 29, 1944. He was an avid Cubs fan and had three dreams as a kid: 1) to pitch in the major leagues; 2) to be a professional organist (he began lessons at age eight); and 3) to be a jet pilot.

When McLain was fifteen, his father died. Although his mother remarried a year later, McLain never got over the loss.

By the time McLain was in high school, he was dominating local baseball teams. After finishing with a 43–6 record for Mt. Carmel High, he signed a professional contract with the Chicago White Sox.

The White Sox sent him to one of their minor league teams in the Appalachian League. In his first professional game, McLain pitched a no-hitter. He walked the first three batters he faced, then relied solely on his fastball to baffle the other team for the remainder of the game.

The Detroit Tigers acquired him the next year, and in September of 1963 McLain made his first major league appearance. As luck would have it, his first start was against the White Sox. McLain made the White Sox sorry they had not kept him as he pitched the Tigers to a 4–3 victory. He even added a home run of his own to cap off the win.

McLain had a repertoire of several pitches, including a fastball, a slider, and a change-up that left batters swinging mightily at empty air. Most of all, though, he had amazing control. In 1968, for example, he gave up only 63 walks in 336 innings.

"Catching McLain was almost like having a night off," said Bill Freehan. "He worked quickly and had a great pitching technique. His control, though, made him special. I'd give him a target to throw to, and I'd hardly have to move the glove at all. The ball would be right there."

McLain won 20 games for the 1966 Tigers, giving a glimpse of the greatness that was to come. One of his most important strengths, a self-confidence that bordered on arrogance, was already in place.

"He was the consummate believer in himself," said Freehan. "I remember one night we were playing in Baltimore. Paul Blair, Frank Robinson, and Brooks Robinson were all on base, with nobody out. I wanted to stall for time so we could get a relief pitcher warmed up, so I walked slowly out to the mound.

" 'What are you dragging yourself out here to tell me that I don't already know?' McLain said. 'Just go back and catch like you're supposed to and I'll get us out of this.'

"I went back to catch and up came Boog Powell, the Orioles' first baseman and one of the most powerful hitters in the league. Powell hit the ball hard, a line drive right at McLain, but he caught the ball and started a triple play to end the inning.

"When we got back to the dugout, McLain came over to me. He just smiled and said, 'Didn't I tell you I would think of something?'"

Another of McLain's teammates, Jim Northrup, provides a different example of the star pitcher's incredible self-confidence. "He was pitching and we were ahead, three to nothing," said Northrup. "He threw a fastball to the batter, who hit a home run. The next batter came up and McLain threw another fastball. The batter hit another home run, making the score three to two.

"McLain struck out the next three batters, all on fastballs. When we got back to the dugout I said, 'Did you ever think about throwing a curveball after those two batters hit home runs off of your fastball?' McLain looked at me and said, 'Let me ask you something. How many times have you ever seen a team hit three home runs in an inning?'"

McLain's supreme self-confidence often annoyed fans and teammates alike. He always did things his own way and he was usually the center of attention, even at the expense of others.

McLain's outspoken comments, frequent as they were, often managed to catch everyone by surprise. He once called the Tigers "a country-club team" (implying that they weren't tough), and he referred to Tiger fans as "the worst in baseball." The fans responded by booing him and the media quickly dubbed him "Mighty Mouth."

"You realize early in your career that all athletes are different," said Freehan. "Just as in everyday life, there are some you get along with better than others. My only concern as a catcher was how McLain performed as a pitcher.

"I never had any trouble with him during close games. He always had good concentration then. When we had a big lead, though, I had to work hard to keep him focused on the game."

McLain stayed focused for all of 1968. He finished the year with a 31–6 record and a 1.96 ERA. He had 280 strikeouts and threw 6 shutouts.

Winning 30 games was much more difficult in 1968 than it had been when Dizzy Dean and Lefty Grove accomplished the feat. You could argue that the competition was tougher in 1968, that athletes were generally more talented as a whole.

The real difference, though, was with the media. The number of newspaper, television, and radio reporters following McLain was much greater than it had been for Dean and Grove. McLain was always being interviewed, which increased the pressure on him (just as it had for Roger Maris when he chased Babe Ruth's home run record in 1961).

But in 1968, McLain responded to the pressure with one of the greatest seasons of all time. Picking an American League Cy Young Award winner that year was easy. The twenty-four-year-old McLain was the unanimous choice.

Controversy always seemed to follow McLain. In his last game that year, the Tigers faced the Yankees. The Tigers had clinched the pennant the previous day, so there was no pressure on them.

New York Yankees legend Mickey Mantle was about to retire. He needed one home run to put him into third place on the all-time list, behind Babe Ruth and Willie Mays and just ahead of Jimmy Foxx.

"Mantle had been a childhood idol of McLain's," said Freehan. "Before the game, McLain had said that he was going to let Mantle hit a home run, provided it wouldn't affect the outcome of the game.

"Sure enough, Mantle comes up to bat toward the end of the game. We already had a big lead, and McLain was going to win his thirty-first game.

"McLain threw Mantle an easy one right down the middle of the plate, and Mantle got his home run. What was funny was listening to their explanations after the game.

"Mantle said, 'Oh, yeah, he definitely wanted me to hit the home run.' McLain, on the other hand, denied everything. 'Oh, no,' he said, 'I would never do anything to tamper with the integrity of the game of baseball.' "

McLain's incredible talent helped lead Detroit to its first pennant in twenty-three years. The Tigers' World Series opponents were the St. Louis

Cardinals, who were led by another Cy Young Award winner, Bob Gibson.

Before the Series began, McLain offered another of his unusually blunt comments. "I want to humiliate the Cardinals," he said. But McLain had pitched 336 innings and 27 complete games that year, and the long season had taken its toll.

"McLain had thrown a lot of innings that year, and you could see how tired he was," said Freehan. "You have to remember that relief pitchers were rarely used in those days. If you started a game, you expected to finish it."

"His arm was tired, and it showed," agreed McLain's teammate Jim Northrup. "He had lost the 'pop' in his fastball, no question about it."

Gibson and McLain were matched in Game 1, but it was no contest. Gibson was in command from the start, and the Cardinals won easily.

Gibson, whom McLain called "the greatest pitcher I've ever seen," beat the Tigers twice in the Series. With the Tigers trailing three games to two, McLain won the crucial sixth game. The next day, Mickey Lolich outpitched Gibson to give the Tigers the championship.

McLain's incredible season made him very popular during the off-season. "The Ed Sullivan Show," "The Steve Allen Show," and "The Smothers Brothers Comedy Hour" were only a few of the people and programs begging for an appearance by McLain.

McLain's greatest love, outside of baseball, was music. He played the organ in the off-season, and gave music lessons during the season. His new celebrity status gave him more opportunities to play his music, and he took advantage of it. Often flying his own plane, he played in clubs that ranged from the more subdued atmosphere of his hometown in Saginaw, Michigan, to the flashy, showier clubs of Las Vegas. He recorded two albums on Capitol Records in 1968: *Denny McLain at the Organ* and *Denny McLain in Las Vegas,* the latter one recorded live.

The celebration of the 1968 season did not wind down until the beginning of the 1969 year. Few people expected another outstanding season from Mclain. Despite his exceptional accomplishments in 1968, the pressure had been constant all year long. No one would have been surprised if McLain had a subpar year.

But McLain defied the skeptics who doubted that he could ever come close to duplicating his 31-win season. Although he didn't win 30, he had another excellent season. He finished the year with 24 wins and only 9 losses, and shared the 1969 Cy Young Award with Baltimore's Mike Cuellar.

That was the last great year for McLain. In 1970, he was suspended by the baseball commissioner for three months for associating with gamblers. He came

COURTESY OF THE DETROIT TIGERS

back out of shape and never regained the pitching form that once made him so dominant. He was suspended two more times that year, once for carrying a weapon and once for pouring a bucket of ice water on two sportswriters.

At the end of the 1970 season, McLain was traded to the Washington Senators, for whom he won 10 games and lost 22 in the 1971 season. He pitched for the Oakland A's and the Atlanta Braves in 1972 before finally retiring.

In 1985, McLain was sent to jail for, among other things, selling cocaine. His conviction was overturned on appeal in 1987, and he was released.

There is no question that Denny McLain led a troubled life at the end of his baseball career and after he retired. But that does not change the fact that, for a few years, he was one of baseball's most dominant pitchers.

"He challenged everybody," said Northrup. "And he only walked someone when he wanted to.

"He had the greatest control and confidence in the game. For two years, he was the best pitcher I ever saw."

Today McLain hosts a radio call-in show in Detroit. He still takes great pride in being the only man in the last sixty years to win 30 games. "I'm the only person alive who has done it," he said. "There are 260 million people who live in this country, and I'm the only one who has won thirty games in a season."

DENNY McLAIN—CAREER STATISTICS

YEAR	CLUB	LEAGUE	G	IP	W	L	H	R	ER	SO	BB	ERA
1963	DETROIT	AMERICAN	3	21	2	1	20	12	10	22	16	4.29
1964	DETROIT	AMERICAN	19	100	4	5	84	48	45	70	37	4.05
1965	DETROIT	AMERICAN	33	220	16	6	174	75	64	192	62	2.61
1966	DETROIT	AMERICAN	38	264	20	14	205	120	115	192	104	3.92
1967	DETROIT	AMERICAN	37	235	17	16	209	110	99	161	73	3.79
1968	DETROIT	AMERICAN	41	336	31	6	241	86	73	280	63	1.96
1969	DETROIT	AMERICAN	42	325	24	9	288	105	101	181	67	2.80
1970	DETROIT	AMERICAN	14	91	3	5	100	51	47	52	68	4.65
1971	WASHINGTON	AMERICAN	33	217	10	22	233	115	103	103	72	4.27
1972	OAKLAND; ATLANTA	(AM.; NAT.)	20	76	4	7	92	17	15	29	26	6.39
MAJOR LEAGUE TOTALS			80	1885	131	91	1646	739	572	1282	548	3.39

4. TOM SEAVER

LEADING A FRANCHISE TO THE TOP

The largest crowd in Shea Stadium history—more than 59,000 fans—cheered every one of Tom Seaver's pitches. The date was July 9, 1969. The New York Mets star was working on a perfect game and needed only three more outs to accomplish one of baseball's most difficult feats.

Seaver was calm as the visiting Chicago Cubs came to bat in the top of the ninth inning. He had overpowered the first-place Cubs all night, striking out 11 batters in the first eight innings. The Mets held a 4–0 lead, but the enthusiastic crowd was looking for more than just a victory.

The first batter to face the twenty-four-year-old right-hander was catcher Randy Hundley. Like the rest of his teammates, Hundley had struggled all night against Seaver. Hundley decided that the element of surprise might help him get on base.

Seaver threw his trademark fastball and the crowd booed angrily as Hundley bunted the ball and sprinted toward first base. Seaver picked up the ball quickly, though, and the crowd roared again as his throw beat Hundley to first base. The Cubs were down to their last two outs.

The next batter was Jim Qualls, a rookie outfielder. He had flied out deep to right field earlier in the game and had also grounded out to the first baseman.

Qualls was batting left-handed, and Seaver wanted to pitch him on the outside part of the plate. But when his fastball drifted inside, Seaver could only watch as Qualls drove the ball into left-center field for a solid base hit.

Seaver's perfect game was over, but the Met fans still rose to their feet to cheer his outstanding performance. The Cubs were still in first place, but the Mets were closing in fast. More important, the Mets were no longer considered the joke of the National League. They had established themselves as legitimate contenders.

And the man responsible for that was Tom Seaver.

The New York Mets joined the National League in 1962, and the club quickly established itself as one of the worst teams in baseball history. After five years of incompetence, most of Seaver's teammates *expected* to lose.

Seaver's arrival in 1967 signified the turnaround of the Mets. In his rookie year, he won 16 games, an amazing feat considering the lack of support his teammates gave him. Seaver was an easy selection for the National League Rookie of the Year.

Seaver won 16 games again the next season. His competitive nature and determination inspired his teammates, who were slowly starting to realize that their team might not have to remain losers forever.

"The 'lovable losers' was not something I was a part of," said Seaver. "I came up in '67 and a number of good young players arrived over the next two to three years—including Buddy Harrelson, Cleon Jones, Jerry Grote, Jerry Koosman, Gary Gentry, and Tug McGraw. We knew the reputation of the previous teams, but we never thought of ourselves as losers at all."

Led by "Tom Terrific," the Mets began to believe in themselves in 1969. Where they used to find ways to lose games, they now began to find ways to win. When St. Louis Cardinals pitcher Steve Carlton struck out 19 Mets to set a major league record, New York still managed to win, 4–3.

On August 15, a month after Seaver's near-perfect game, the Mets trailed the first-place Chicago Cubs by 9½ games. But inspired by Seaver, New York refused to quit. They kept winning, and clinched the Eastern Division title on September 24.

The long-suffering fans at Shea celebrated by rushing onto the field and taking home bases and

COURTESY OF THE NEW YORK METS

clumps of sod as souvenirs of the momentous occasion. For the first time, the Mets were winners.

"We knew we would be competitive that year," said Seaver. "But I don't think we actually believed we could win it all, though, until it happened."

New York's National League Championship Series opponent was the Atlanta Braves. The winner would go to the World Series. Seaver, although not at his best, won the first game against Atlanta. The Mets then won the next two games and headed to the World Series to face the powerful Baltimore Orioles.

Many people wondered if the Mets had gone as far as they could go, and the Orioles tried to answer that question immediately. In Game 1, on Seaver's second pitch, Oriole Don Buford blasted a home run. The Orioles coasted to an easy 4–1 win.

The Mets came back to win the next two games, and Seaver was on the mound again for Game 4. He pitched brilliantly and took a 1–0 lead into the ninth inning.

Baltimore tied it in the ninth, and only a diving catch by outfielder Ron Swoboda prevented the Orioles from taking the lead. Seaver held Baltimore scoreless in the top of the tenth inning. In the bottom of the tenth, with Mets on first and second, J. C. Martin pinch-hit for Seaver. Martin bunted the ball and Orioles pitcher Pete Richert tried to throw him out at first. But Richert's throw hit Martin's wrist and, before the Orioles could retrieve the ball, the Mets had scored the winning run.

The Mets finished off the Orioles in Game 5, winning the Series four games to one. Seaver and the "Amazin' Mets" were world champions.

Seaver was baseball's best pitcher that year, winning 25 games while losing only 7. He had winning streaks of 8 and 10 games, and struck out 208 batters while compiling an ERA of 2.21.

Seaver was an easy winner of that year's Cy Young Award. He also captured several other honors for his role in the Mets' amazing season, including being named *Sports Illustrated*'s Sportsman of the Year. He finished second to the Giants' Willie McCovey in the Most Valuable Player voting.

"McCovey was one of the two most difficult batters I ever faced—the other was Pittsburgh's Willie Stargell," said Seaver. "Both were low-fastball hitters, which was my strength.

"I was a pitcher that would pitch with my strength, as opposed to pitching to a hitter's weakness. If they could hit my strength—and McCovey and Stargell could—more power to them."

For Seaver, winning the Cy Young Award must be put in perspective. "The Cy Young Award stands on its own merits; it is a real personal achievement," said Seaver. "But when you win a championship like we did in '69, that's a much greater feeling than winning an individual award. The championship is something you can share with your teammates, and it's something you can share for a lifetime. "

George Thomas Seaver was born on November 17, 1944, in Fresno, California. He was the fourth child in a very athletic family. Seaver's father was an excellent amateur golfer who, in 1930, came within one stroke of winning a semifinal match that would have enabled him to meet the legendary Bobby Jones for the U.S. Amateur title.

Seaver's interest in baseball was apparent at an early age. As a three-year-old, he would entertain himself for hours in his backyard by playing imaginary baseball.

By the age of eight, Seaver's skills were so advanced that he was able to compete with boys several years older. Little League teams wanted him on their clubs, but he was rejected because he was too young. When he was finally old enough to play, he dominated his league immediately.

Other sports also appealed to Seaver. At Fresno High, he starred in both basketball and baseball. He was an All-City forward in basketball, and his father believes he could have played in college.

After graduating, he spent six months with the Marines and six months working at his father's fruit-packing plant. The combination of hard work and Mother Nature helped to dramatically change Seaver's body during the year following graduation. He grew four inches and added forty-five pounds of muscle, becoming a powerful 6'1", 190 pounds.

Following one year at Fresno City College, Seaver's baseball ability won him a scholarship to play for the University of Southern California (USC), a school well known for its baseball teams. "I don't think I realized that baseball was 'it' for me—at least in terms of possibly playing professionally—until I got to USC," said Seaver. "Even when I went to junior college, I was still thinking about junior college basketball. Finally, at USC, I began to feel that I would have a chance of making it as a pro."

Following an excellent season at USC, Seaver was drafted by the Los Angeles Dodgers. But the Dodgers made no attempt to sign him, so Seaver remained at USC.

The Atlanta Braves drafted Seaver the next year, but waited too long to sign him. Seaver and USC had already started their season. Under baseball's agreement with the colleges, professional teams were not permitted to sign a player who was currently playing on a college team. When Seaver finally accepted the Braves' offer, he had already pitched in two games for USC.

By signing the contract with the Braves, Seaver forfeited his college eligibility. But when the Braves were denied the rights to Seaver for violating baseball's agreement with the colleges, Seaver found himself in an odd position. He was neither a college player nor a professional player.

Seaver took it upon himself to write a letter to the baseball commissioner at that time, William Eckert. In the letter, Seaver explained how unfair his situation was.

The commissioner agreed, and stated that any team willing to match the Braves' offer could sign Seaver. The Mets, Phillies, and Indians expressed interest in Seaver, and the commissioner put all three of their names in a hat. A drawing was held, and the Mets were the lucky winners.

"It was good for Seaver to go to the Mets," said Commissioner Eckert years later. "They were a young team that was not doing well, and Seaver was given the opportunity to help them quickly."

Whereas most major leaguers spent several years in the minors, Seaver's one and only minor league season was spent with the Mets' AAA team in Jacksonville, Florida. Following a 12–12 year, he headed for the major leagues, where he remained for more than twenty years.

Seaver tied a major league record for strikeouts in 1970 when he struck out 19 batters in a game against the San Diego Padres. With two outs in the sixth inning, Seaver had only 9 strikeouts. From that point on, however, he struck out a record 10 consecutive batters to tie the single-game strikeout record.

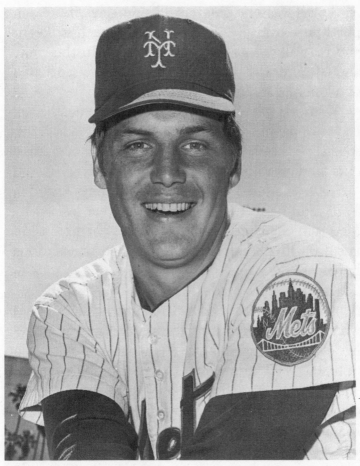

Although Seaver recalls that game, he doesn't rate it as his most memorable. "When you play for over twenty years, there are a lot of games and memories," he said.

"There was one game in Los Angeles, for example. I pitched twelve innings, with sixteen strikeouts and no walks. I gave up one run early in the game, and left after the twelfth inning with the score tied, one–one. I got a no-decision.

"It's not a game that anyone would remember except the people who were there. But it was a very special performance—twelve innings, sixteen strikeouts, and no walks."

Seaver captured his second Cy Young Award in 1973, and his 19–10 record for the year helped the Mets win their second World Series championship. His 2.08 ERA and 251 strikeouts led the National League.

Seaver overpowered hitters with his fastball, particularly in the early years. "You almost always knew what was coming against Seaver in the early days, because he would always challenge you with that fastball," said former St. Louis Cardinals catcher Tim McCarver, who is now a broadcaster. "You could just never seem to get on top of that fastball, it kept going up, up, up. He certainly was the most difficult pitcher I ever tried to hit."

Following a disappointing 11–11 season in 1974, Seaver won 22 games for the 1975 Mets. His 243 strikeouts again led the league, and he won his third Cy Young Award.

"As your career progresses, you really begin to develop a respect for your trade," said Seaver. "And you begin to understand that it is a continual learning process. Learning what it takes to throw a certain pitch, learning what to do in a certain situation. If you do things correctly, the way they're supposed to be done, then over the course of time you're going to win."

In the middle of the 1977 season, following a contract dispute with the Mets, the unthinkable happened: Seaver was traded to the Cincinnati Reds. "It was a bittersweet departure," he said. "I hated leaving the guys I was playing with, but it was time for me to go.

"The Mets organization was a shambles, and I was getting a lot of the blame for things that were going on. I am a loyal person, but my loyalties were used against me in a very underhanded way. It was time to leave, and get on with my career."

Seaver continued to be successful during his five and a half years with the Reds, but it was hard for the fans to see him in anything but a Mets uniform. In 1978, he pitched his only no-hitter in a 4–0 shutout over the St. Louis Cardinals.

He was arguably baseball's best pitcher in 1981, when he compiled a 14–2 record in the strike-shortened season. Seaver narrowly missed winning his fourth Cy Young Award that year when he was edged out by the charismatic star of the Los Angeles Dodgers, Fernando Valenzuela. Always the competitor, Seaver feels the balloting that year was unfair.

"There were two writers in San Diego who didn't believe I deserved a first-, second-, or third-place vote," Seaver said. "You try to figure it out from a logical point of view. I can't."

In 1983, Seaver returned to the Mets for one more season and finished with a 9–14 record. He signed with the Chicago White Sox of the American League in 1984, and all of baseball watched as he slowly closed in on one of the sport's rarest accomplishments—300 career victories.

As fate would have it, Seaver's three hundredth victory occurred in New York, in a game against the Yankees. Seaver was no longer with the Mets, but New York fans were still thrilled to have the opportunity to cheer their hero once more.

"That day was the culmination of a goal that comes into focus at the end of your career," he said. "All of a sudden, out of all the thousands of people who have played the game of baseball, you've got a chance to join only a handful that ever won three hundred games.

"It meant so much to be back in New York, in front of all the people who had supported me for ten years. I had my father there, my family, my friends.

"I could probably give you a memorable game for

every town I pitched in. But if I had to select a single game as my most memorable one, that would be it."

Seaver's final season was with the Boston Red Sox in 1986. Although he was injured late in the year and missed the playoffs and World Series, he is credited with providing stability and guidance to the young Boston pitching staff.

"I had played for [Boston manager] John McNamara in Cincinnati, and he knew exactly what he was getting: a solid starter who could add some professionalism to his young pitching staff," said Seaver. "It never hurts to have a veteran with a good work ethic who knows about winning.

"A lot of that is overlooked today. They teach kids how to play, but you've also got to teach them how to win. It's one of the most overlooked aspects of baseball."

Seaver retired at the end of the 1986 season. In the winter of 1992, he was elected to the Baseball Hall of Fame. He was named on 98.9 percent of the ballots, the highest percentage in the history of the voting.

The annual ceremony takes place each summer in Cooperstown, New York. And, although there were others inducted at the same time as Seaver—relief pitcher Rollie Fingers, umpire Bill McGowan, and pitcher Hal Newhouser—the crowd of 20,000 was there to see one person.

"Seaver! Seaver! Seaver!" they chanted, even be-

TOM SEAVER—CAREER STATISTICS

YEAR	CLUB	LEAGUE	G	IP	W	L	H	R	ER	SO	BB	ERA
1966	JACKSONVILLE	INTERNATIONAL	34	210	12	12	184	87	73	188	66	3.13
1967	NEW YORK	NATIONAL	35	251	16	13	224	85	77	170	78	2.76
1968	NEW YORK	NATIONAL	36	278	16	12	224	73	68	205	48	2.20
1969	NEW YORK	NATIONAL	36	273	25	7	202	75	67	208	82	2.21
1970	NEW YORK	NATIONAL	37	291	18	12	230	103	91	283	83	2.81
1971	NEW YORK	NATIONAL	36	286	20	10	210	61	56	289	61	1.76
1972	NEW YORK	NATIONAL	35	262	21	12	215	92	85	249	77	2.92
1973	NEW YORK	NATIONAL	36	290	19	10	219	74	67	251	64	2.08
1974	NEW YORK	NATIONAL	32	236	11	11	199	89	84	201	75	3.20
1975	NEW YORK	NATIONAL	36	280	22	9	217	81	74	243	88	2.38
1976	NEW YORK	NATIONAL	35	271	14	11	211	83	78	235	77	2.59
1977	NEW YORK–CINCINNATI	NATIONAL	33	261	21	6	199	78	75	196	66	2.59
1978	CINCINNATI	NATIONAL	36	260	16	14	218	97	83	226	89	2.87

Year	Team	League										
1979	CINCINNATI	NATIONAL	32	215	16	6	187	85	75	131	61	3.14
1980	CINCINNATI	NATIONAL	26	168	10	8	140	74	68	101	59	3.64
1981	CINCINNATI	NATIONAL	23	166	14	2	120	51	47	87	66	2.55
1982	CINCINNATI	NATIONAL	21	111.1	5	13	136	75	68	62	44	5.50
1983	NEW YORK	NATIONAL	34	231	9	14	201	104	91	135	86	3.55
1984	CHICAGO	AMERICAN	34	236.2	15	11	216	108	104	131	61	3.95
1985	CHICAGO	AMERICAN	35	238.2	16	11	223	103	84	134	69	3.17
1986	CHICAGO—BOSTON	AMERICAN	28	176.1	7	13	180	83	79	103	56	4.03
MAJOR LEAGUE TOTALS (20 YEARS)			656	4782	311	205	3971	1674	1521	3640	1390	2.86

fore he was introduced. When he was finally intro-duced and stepped to the podium, the crowd roared with joy and gave him a standing ovation.

Yankee Stadium was known as "The House That Ruth Built." It could easily be said that Seaver meant as much to the Mets as Ruth did to the Yankees.

"Seaver was the quintessential Mets player," said Tim McCarver. "There is no question that he was the most important player in the history of their franchise."

5. BOB GIBSON

AN UNMATCHED COMPETITIVE SPIRIT

I t was the confrontation the fans had paid to see. Batting for the Pittsburgh Pirates in this July 1967 game was star right fielder Roberto Clemente. Pitching for the St. Louis Cardinals was Bob Gibson, whose unmatched competitive spirit made him one of the greatest pitchers in baseball history.

Gibson loved matchups with other teams' stars. He was driven to prove he was better than everyone he faced, particularly future Hall of Famers like Clemente.

Gibson tried to throw his trademark fastball past Clemente, but Clemente hit the ball hard. The crack of the bat meeting the ball was quickly followed by another crack, that of the ball smashing into Gibson's shin. Gibson fell to the ground in agony.

Although in obvious pain, he refused to leave the game. He struggled to his feet and pitched to two more batters before the pain became more than he could bear. At the hospital, X rays showed that Gibson had continued pitching with a broken leg.

Gibson was expected to miss the remainder of the season. Amazingly, though, he returned in six weeks, his pitching and inspiration helping the Cardinals win the National League pennant.

"He was the most intense competitor I ever played with," said his former catcher, Tim McCarver. "Not only did he have enormous ability, he had an even stronger, burning desire to win."

As good as Gibson was in 1967, he was even better in 1968. Not only did he win the Cy Young Award, he was also named the league's Most Valuable Player. In winning the MVP, he captured 14 of the 20 votes cast by the Baseball Writers Association of America; the other 6 votes went to Cincinnati Reds star Pete Rose.

Gibson won 22 games and lost 9 for the Cardinals in 1968, helping them capture another National League pennant. He pitched 13 shutouts and allowed only one run in 9 other games. He had 268 strikeouts, and his ERA was a National League record 1.12 (still the lowest for a National League Cy Young Award winner). His performance that year is considered one of the best single seasons of all time.

Another statistic highlighted Gibson's importance to the Cardinals and his domination of opposing batters. Gibson completed 28 of his 34 starts in 1968 and was lifted for a pinch hitter in the other 6. He

was never removed from the game while he was actually pitching.

"He was phenomenal that year," said former
Cardinals manager Red Schoendienst. "Every pitch
he threw seemed to have something extra on it. He
also had great control, and could throw the ball high
and inside or low and away. He was hard to hit and
hard to beat.

"If we had a two- or three-game losing streak, it
was great to see him going out to pitch. You knew
that there was a very good chance he'd put the team
back on the right track."

Gibson led the Cardinals into the 1968 World Series against the Detroit Tigers. Detroit's star was
Denny McLain, winner of 31 games and the American League Cy Young Award.

Game one featured a duel between the two Cy
Young Award winners, but the Cardinals were confident. "We weren't nervous about facing McLain,"
said Tim McCarver. "You were never worried about
another pitcher when you had Gibson."

Additionally, Gibson relished the thought of
showing the world that he was better than McLain,
despite McLain's 31 wins. McLain gave Gibson and
the Cardinals greater incentive when he was quoted
as saying Detroit would "humiliate" St. Louis.

Gibson took command of Game 1 from the beginning. By the ninth inning, the Cardinals were lead-

ing 4–0 and Gibson had struck out 14 batters. He overpowered the Tigers in the ninth, striking out the side to give him a Series-record 17 strikeouts, and the Cardinals the victory. (The World Series record for strikeouts in a single game had been established by Sandy Koufax in 1963 when he struck out 15 against the New York Yankees.)

"Gibson had that exploding fastball and a slider that broke extremely well," said McCarver. "In fact, the Tigers' Willie Horton still can't believe he wasn't hit by the pitch he struck out on to end Gibson's seventeen-strikeouts World Series game. I remember Horton groaning loudly because he thought Gibson's pitch was about to hit him. But then the ball broke sharply for a strike and the game was over."

Robert Gibson was born November 9, 1935, in Omaha, Nebraska. His family was very poor. His father died a month before he was born and his mother held two jobs, working both as a maid and in a Laundromat.

Gibson was a natural athlete. He was a basketball and track star for Omaha Technical High School, and excelled in baseball on the Nebraska sandlots.

Gibson wanted to pursue basketball in college, but neither of his first choices, Indiana University and the University of Nebraska, offered him a scholarship. The reason for this, Gibson thought, was that he was black. Angry, he vowed to find a school where he could prove himself at the next level of competition.

He finally accepted an athletic scholarship to Creighton University in Nebraska, where he became the first black player on both the basketball and baseball teams. He excelled in both sports, just as he did in high school.

In 1957, Gibson decided to leave Creighton and signed not one, but two professional contracts. He agreed to play baseball for the St. Louis Cardinals and he also signed a contract to play basketball with the Harlem Globetrotters. The Globetrotters combined great basketball ability with trick plays, and their entertaining style delighted audiences all over the world.

Although Gibson played a conservative game for the Globetrotters, he was able to dribble behind his back and perform some other plays that were considered flashy in those days. After one year, though, the Cardinals insisted that he concentrate on baseball. They were worried that Gibson might suffer a career-ending injury on the basketball court.

Gibson reluctantly agreed to make baseball his one and only sport. Although he loved basketball, he often suffered from severe asthma attacks, and baseball would be less of a physical strain on his body than the constant running demanded by basketball.

From 1957 through 1960, Gibson pitched for the

Cardinals' minor league teams in Omaha, Columbus (Georgia), and Rochester (New York). He also made brief appearances in the major leagues with the Cardinals in 1959 and 1960, before establishing himself as a permanent big leaguer in 1961.

Gibson was wild early in his career, which, combined with his blazing fastball, made for many a nervous batter in the National League. Batters also knew that Gibson was known to throw at batters and, frequently, to hit them. No one wanted to be hit by a Gibson fastball.

"Bob wasn't just unfriendly when he pitched," said Joe Torre, who played with him on the Cardinals. "I'd say it was more like hateful."

Chicago Cubs Hall of Fame outfielder Billy Williams put it another way: "He looked at you like you were trying to take bread off his table."

"A lot of players on the opposing teams tried to get friendly with Gibson," said Schoendienst. "But he wouldn't speak to anybody. He was afraid he would become a less effective pitcher if he became too friendly.

"He also worked hard to keep every advantage he had. For example, he liked to throw a hard sinker if he needed to get someone to hit into a double play. But after the game, if a writer asked him what pitch he threw to get a key out, he'd always say the same thing: 'Fastball.' "

Gibson established himself as one of the league's

best pitchers in 1963, when he won 18 games and lost only 9. In 1964 he won 19 games, including 9 of his last 11. His victory on the final day of the season helped the Cards win the pennant by a single game over the second-place Phillies and Reds.

"You can't say enough about him," said Schoendienst. "When you have a guy on your team that battled as hard as Gibson did, it just makes the rest of the team fight that much harder.

"He was driven to win," Schoendienst continued, "and would do whatever it took to reach that goal. If he had to strike out a lot of batters to win, he'd do that. If he had to hit a home run, he'd do that."

Gibson's 1964 heroics led the Cardinals into the World Series against the New York Yankees. In Game 7, pitching on only two days' rest, he struck out nine while leading the Cardinals to a 7–5 win and the world championship. He also struck out a record 31 batters in the Series, breaking the sixty-one-year-old record of Boston Red Sox pitcher Bill Dineen.

Gibson was an impatient person, a trait that affected his pitching. Unlike today's pitchers, who dawdle between every pitch, Gibson liked to throw his pitches in rapid succession.

He could also be impatient with his manager, particularly if he was being removed from a game. "I didn't usually go out to the mound to tell him anything," said Schoendienst. "I might go out just to give him a chance to catch his breath. The few times I had to take him out of a game, he'd never say anything, but you could see how angry he was."

Gibson's impatience applied to the media, as well. He had little respect for the press, particularly if he judged a question foolish. Reporters learned quickly that they had better have all their facts before they interviewed Gibson; otherwise, it would be a very short interview.

Gibson loved the mental aspects of pitching, the challenge each batter offered. "There's so much to think about out there," he said. "It's all about concentration."

"He'd think everything out the day before he pitched," said Schoendienst. "When he came to the park the next day, he knew exactly what he wanted to do and how he was going to do it."

Gibson looked for challenges in other aspects of the game besides pitching. While other pitchers were content to do some light running or casually chase fly balls during batting practice, Gibson spent much of his time playing third base. He relished the challenge of proving that his athletic ability included more than just pitching. Still, Cardinals management became very nervous every time they thought about what a bad bounce at third base could do to their ace pitcher.

Gibson pitched with a unique motion that ended with his right foot falling off to the left side of the

pitching mound. His unusual style appeared to leave him ill-prepared to catch balls that were hit his way. Despite this seemingly awkward motion, though, he was one of the best fielding pitchers in the game.

In the 1964 World Series, for example, Gibson was pitching to Joe Pepitone in the ninth inning of Game 5. The Cards led by two runs, there was one out, and Mickey Mantle was on first base.

Pepitone hit a line drive off Gibson's hip, and the ball rolled toward third base, away from the direction of Gibson's natural follow-through. Gibson recovered quickly, though, and somehow managed to throw out Pepitone.

The next batter, Tom Tresh, hit a two-run home run to tie the game. Were it not for Gibson's spectacular fielding ability, the Yankees would have won the game on Tresh's homer. Instead, the Cardinals went on to win the game in extra innings.

Few pitchers could match Gibson's skill as a batter. While most pitchers consider themselves fortunate to bat much more than .100 for a season, Gibson's *career* batting average was .206. He also hit with power, and finished with 24 career home runs.

"He was a dangerous hitter because he could hit the ball out of the park," said Schoendienst. "If nothing else, he felt that if he stayed in the game long enough, he would come up to bat and hit a home run."

Gibson won 20 games for the Cardinals again in

1969. He followed that with another outstanding year in 1970, winning 23 games while losing only 7. His excellent season earned him his second Cy Young Award in three years.

The 1970 season would be the last year Gibson would win 20 games. He won 16 in 1971, including a no-hitter against Pittsburgh, and followed with 19 more wins in 1972.

But the end of his career was approaching fast. After winning 12 games in 1973 and 11 in 1974, he could manage only 3 wins and 10 losses in 1975. The time had come to retire.

Gibson always loved challenges, and there was none greater than the World Series. Gibson proved himself so many times in the Fall Classic that it could be argued that he was the best World Series pitcher in baseball history. Pitching in three Series, he posted a 7–2 record that included 7 straight victories, 8 complete games, 92 strikeouts, and an ERA of 1.89.

In addition to his strikeout record for a Series, Gibson is the only pitcher to win two seventh games. He first accomplished the feat in the 1964 Series, winning the final game against the Yankees despite pitching on only two days' rest. In the 1967 Series against the Boston Red Sox, he won Game 7 by a 7–2 score, striking out 10 and even hitting a home run.

Gibson played 17 years in the major leagues and finished with a record of 251–174. He was also one

of the game's great strikeout pitchers. He struck out
200 or more batters in nine seasons, and 260 or more
batters in four seasons. He finished his career with a
total of 3,117 strikeouts, ranking him ninth on the
all-time list.

Gibson was elected to the Hall of Fame in 1981.
He became only the eleventh man voted in during
his first season of eligibility (not counting the origi-
nal inductees), a tribute to both his talent and his
enormous desire to win.

"He was more than just a great competitor; he also
had great talent," said Schoendienst. "To put it simply, he was just hard to beat."

BOB GIBSON—CAREER STATISTICS

YEAR	CLUB	LEAGUE	G	IP	W	L	H	R	ER	SO	BB	ERA
1957	OMAHA	AMER. ASSOC.	10	42	2	1	46	26	20	25	27	4.29
1957	COLUMBUS	SALLY	8	43	4	3	36	26	18	24	34	3.77
1958	OMAHA	AMER. ASSOC.	13	87	3	4	79	45	32	47	39	3.31
1958	ROCHESTER	INTERNATIONAL	20	103	5	5	88	35	28	75	54	2.45
1959	OMAHA	AMER. ASSOC.	24	135	9	9	128	59	46	98	70	3.07
1959	ST. LOUIS	NATIONAL	13	76	3	5	77	35	28	48	39	3.32
1960	ST. LOUIS	NATIONAL	27	87	3	6	97	61	54	69	48	5.59
1960	ROCHESTER	INTERNATIONAL	6	41	2	3	33	15	13	36	17	2.85
1961	ST. LOUIS	NATIONAL	35	211	13	12	186	91	76	166	119	3.24
1962	ST. LOUIS	NATIONAL	32	234	15	13	174	84	74	208	95	2.85
1963	ST. LOUIS	NATIONAL	36	255	18	9	224	110	96	204	96	3.39

1964	St. Louis	National	40	287	19	12	250	106	96	245	86	3.01
1965	St. Louis	National	38	299	20	12	243	110	102	270	103	3.07
1966	St. Louis	National	35	280	21	12	210	90	76	225	78	2.44
1967	St. Louis	National	24	175	13	7	151	62	58	147	40	2.98
1968	St. Louis	National	34	305	22	9	198	49	38	268	62	1.12
1969	St. Louis	National	35	314	20	13	251	84	76	269	95	2.18
1970	St. Louis	National	34	294	23	7	262	111	102	274	88	3.12
1971	St. Louis	National	31	246	16	13	215	96	83	185	76	3.04
1972	St. Louis	National	34	278	19	11	226	83	76	208	88	2.46
1973	St. Louis	National	25	195	12	10	159	71	60	142	57	2.77
1974	St. Louis	National	33	240	11	13	236	111	102	129	104	3.83
1975	St. Louis	National	22	109	3	10	120	66	61	60	62	5.04
MAJOR LEAGUE TOTALS			**528**	**3885**	**251**	**174**	**3279**	**1420**	**1258**	**3117**	**1336**	**2.91**

6. JIM PALMER

CONSISTENCY AND GRACE

In the 1966 World Series, twenty-year-old Baltimore Oriole pitcher Jim Palmer was scheduled to start against the National League champion Los Angeles Dodgers and his idol, Sandy Koufax. It was rare for one as young as Palmer to start a World Series game, the ultimate in baseball pressure. To make matters worse, he was facing Koufax, the most dominant pitcher in the game.

Koufax had dominated baseball for the previous five seasons. He had already won two Cy Young Awards, and would claim his third one following the World Series. There was no better pitcher in all of baseball, and Palmer was about to go up against him.

Before the game Palmer jokingly said, "I'll probably have to throw a shutout to beat him." No one believed he could accomplish such a dramatic feat. The Orioles would be happy if he simply managed to keep the score close.

But Palmer stunned everyone by becoming the

USED BY PERMISSION OF THE BALTIMORE ORIOLES

youngest player to ever throw a World Series shut-out. He held the Dodgers to only four hits and struck out six as the Orioles won easily, 6–0.

Koufax retired from baseball the following month. Looking back at that World Series game, one can almost see the crown of pitching greatness being passed from Sandy Koufax to Jim Palmer.

James Alvin Palmer was born on October 15, 1945, in New York City. He does not know his biological parents, but he was adopted by Moe and Polly Wiesen.

Palmer's father died when he was nine, and the family moved to California. Mrs. Wiesen eventually married Max Palmer, and Jim took his stepfather's name in 1959.

Like most superstars, Palmer excelled in many different sports and made them all look easy. For example, in his junior year in high school—his first season on the football team—Palmer caught 54 passes and was named an All-State receiver.

Palmer also excelled at baseball and basketball in high school. In baseball, his high, rising fastball overpowered the young hitters he faced and labeled him as a big-league prospect.

But basketball might have been his best sport. He averaged more than 25 points a game and was again named All-State. Palmer's skills caught the attention of growing college basketball power UCLA and their coach, John Wooden. UCLA offered Palmer a basketball scholarship, but the lure of professional baseball was too much for him to resist and he signed with the Orioles. Had he gone to UCLA, he would have played with Lew Alcindor (later known as Kareem Abdul-Jabbar), who led UCLA to three national titles.

In 1964, his first year in professional baseball, Palmer won 11 games while losing only 3 for the Aberdeen (Maryland) Pheasants in the Northern League. The Orioles were so impressed that they brought him up to the major leagues the following year, an unusual promotion for someone so young. Palmer was a reliever in 1965, but he became a starting pitcher in 1966 and finished the season with a very promising 15–10 record, capped off by his World Series shutout of the Dodgers.

Palmer seemed poised to take off as one of the league's best pitchers. He had youth, size (6'3", 195 pounds), talent, and determination. But he also had a fragile body.

Injuries haunted him for the next two years. His arm, his hip, his back, his shoulder—all gave him trouble at one time or another. The Orioles sent him back down to the minor leagues, in the hope that he would regain his form.

But the pain in his arm was unbearable, and Palmer could barely throw, even at the minor league level. In the minor leagues, he won only one game while losing three. By the end of 1968, even teams that desperately needed pitching were not interested in him. That year, both Kansas City and Seattle elected not to take him in the expansion draft.

In the winter of 1968, Palmer pitched in the Puerto Rican League. Slowly his arm began to get better and he began to regain the confidence that had been nearly destroyed the previous two years.

Palmer returned to the Orioles in 1969, firing the same fastball that had blanked the Dodgers in the 1966 World Series. He finished the season with a superb 16–4 record, highlighted by a no-hitter against the Oakland Athletics. Only six weeks on the disabled list—the result of a separated hip muscle—prevented him from winning 20 games for the first time.

A healthy Palmer finally became a 20-game winner in 1970, the first of four consecutive seasons in which he would accomplish the feat. His new durability enabled him to pitch a league-high 305 innings. He ended the year with two postseason victories, one against Minnesota in the league championship series, the other against Cincinnati in the World Series.

Palmer's pitching motion was smooth and graceful, and was considered the best in baseball. He appeared to be throwing the ball without effort, which made his fastball deceptively fast. Hitters were usually surprised by how quickly his pitches reached them.

Although he struck out a lot of batters, he preferred to let them hit the ball. He believed this saved wear and tear on his arm and allowed him to pitch longer and more effectively. And he had some of the best fielders in the game to help him on defense: Brooks Robinson at third, Mark Belanger at shortstop, and Paul Blair in center field. All three were among the best at their positions, and Palmer was smart enough to rely on their fielding ability.

Palmer was known to have an incredible memory, a talent that undoubtedly helped him decide which pitch to throw a particular batter. His memory was so good that he could recite, pitch by pitch, games played years before.

Palmer won 20 more games in 1971 as a part of what is arguably the best starting pitching staff of all time. All four Oriole starters—Dave McNally, Mike Cuellar, Pat Dobson, and Palmer—won 20 or more games. It was rare for a team to have even two 20-game winners, let alone four of them.

After winning 21 games in 1972, Palmer was 22–9 in 1973, his first Cy Young season. His 2.40 ERA led the American League.

Palmer was recognized for more than his baseball ability. He was as handsome as he was talented. He was also warm and intelligent, and this combination of traits made him an advertiser's dream. In one of the more unusual endorsements for an athlete, Palmer quickly became famous outside the baseball world for his modeling work in a series of underwear ads.

Palmer's 1974 season was the complete opposite of 1973. Slowed by a pinched elbow nerve, Palmer's record fell to a disastrous 7–12. At one point he lost seven consecutive games. He had never before dropped more than three straight.

The elbow injury finally put him on the disabled list. Palmer considered surgery, but the pain began to subside after three weeks. Although he returned to competition after a six-week absence, his arm never felt completely normal that season.

Even more than most pitchers, Palmer did everything possible to protect his pitching arm. He avoided air-conditioning whenever possible, and he always slept with a shirt on to keep his arm warm. Additionally, he made sure to sleep on his left side, thus protecting his right arm. Palmer went so far as to put pillows behind his back to remind him not to roll over onto his right side. He even learned to play tennis left-handed and spent his free time gardening, a hobby he pursued primarily with his left hand.

Palmer was determined to regain his pitching form in 1975 and underwent a rigorous off-season conditioning program. His efforts paid off. He captured his second Cy Young Award after tying for the league

USED BY PERMISSION OF THE BALTIMORE ORIOLES

lead with 23 wins. He had a 2.09 ERA and led the majors with 10 shutouts. His 25 complete games were second best in the American League, and he also struck out 193 batters.

In 1975, Palmer added a major weapon to his pitching abilities: pinpoint control. In 1973, he walked 113 batters while striking out 158, a very high walks-to-strikeouts ratio for a 20-game winner. In 1975, he struck out 193 while walking only 80.

Palmer attributed his new control to experience. "When I first came up," he told *Sports Illustrated*, "all I did was worry about throwing the ball over the plate. I'd get behind the hitters, then have to come down the middle, and balls down the middle are the hardest hit. Location is the key. It's silly to throw pitches out of the strike zone. The important thing is to stay ahead of the hitters. You must use the corners of the plate.

"I can't throw as hard as I used to, so I asked: If I threw all that good before, how did I get hit? The answer is I never thought about the corners. Now I'm putting the ball where I want."

In 1976, Palmer became the first American League pitcher to win three Cy Young Awards (Koufax and Seaver had already accomplished the feat in the National League). He led the league in wins (22) and innings pitched (315), threw 23 complete games (second in the league), and finished the year with a 2.51 ERA.

Palmer's three Cy Young Awards were won over just four years. His domination over this period paralleled the Cy Young streak of Sandy Koufax, who also won three Cy Youngs over four years, 1963–1966.

Palmer was almost as well known for his relationship with Orioles manager Earl Weaver as he was for his pitching skills. Weaver managed Palmer for fifteen years, and he could be every bit as stubborn and outspoken as his ace pitcher.

Though each respected the other's ability, both pitcher and manager were frustrated when they did not get exactly what they wanted. This frequently led to noisy, public confrontations.

A perfect example occurred in a game Palmer was pitching against the Texas Rangers. According to Donald Honig in his book *The Greatest Pitchers of All Time*, Palmer had just given up a double when Weaver rushed out to the mound to yell at him for throwing the wrong pitch. Palmer, equally annoyed with Weaver, handed his glove to the manager and said, "Here, you pitch if you can do better."

The Palmer-Weaver relationship was summed up best in *Sports Illustrated*. "You must never forget that playing baseball is an extension of your youth," said Palmer. "Instead of having my parents scream at me, now I have Earl Weaver."

Despite the distractions of his ongoing battles with Weaver, Palmer proved one of baseball's most consistent pitchers. He won 20 games in 1977 and 21 more in 1978, his eighth 20-win season.

As his career progressed, Palmer became known as the unofficial coach of the Orioles pitching staff. It was a role he enjoyed, and he willingly offered tips and suggestions that the younger pitchers on the staff eagerly absorbed.

After 1978, Palmer's victories came less frequently. Still, he managed to win 16 games in 1980 and 15 in 1982.

In 1983 Palmer was beset by tendinitis in his pitching arm. Following several weeks of rest and rehabilitation, Palmer went to the Orioles' Class A team in Hagerstown, Maryland, to test his arm in game conditions. The last time he had pitched at that level had been 1964, his first year as a professional.

Palmer had two successful outings with Hagerstown and soon returned to Baltimore. He finished the year with a 5–4 record for the Orioles. But after starting the next year 0–3, the thirty-eight-year-old Palmer realized that it was time to retire.

Palmer finished his career as the Orioles' all-time winningest pitcher, with 268 victories, despite missing almost two years with injuries. His winning percentage of .638 is one of baseball's best. He also had 2,212 career strikeouts, a lifetime ERA of 2.86, and is the only pitcher to win World Series games in three different decades.

Palmer was always very modest and never seemed quite comfortable with his fame. Perhaps his early experience with career-threatening injuries made him realize how fragile athletic success can be. He was realistic enough to know that the next injury could be just one pitch away.

But, through hard work and determination, Palmer was always able to overcome his injuries. The man who, as a young pitcher, had idolized Sandy Koufax had now joined him as one of baseball's all-time greats.

JIM PALMER—CAREER STATISTICS

YEAR	CLUB	LEAGUE	G	IP	W	L	H	R	ER	SO	BB	ERA
1964	ABERDEEN	NORTHERN	19	129	11	3	75	42	36	107	130	2.51
1965	BALTIMORE	AMERICAN	27	92	5	4	75	49	38	75	56	3.72
1966	BALTIMORE	AMERICAN	30	208	15	10	176	83	80	147	91	3.46
1967	BALTIMORE	AMERICAN	9	49	3	1	34	18	16	23	20	2.94
1967	ROCHESTER	INTERNATIONAL	2	7	0	0	12	9	9	6	5	11.57
1967	MIAMI	FLORIDA ST.	5	27	1	1	20	6	6	16	10	2.00
1968	MIAMI	FLORIDA ST.	2	8	0	0	4	2	0	5	9	0.00
1968	ROCHESTER	INTERNATIONAL	2	4	0	0	4	6	6	6	8	13.50
1968	ELMIRA	EASTERN	6	25	0	2	18	13	12	26	19	4.32
1969	BALTIMORE	AMERICAN	26	181	16	4	131	48	47	123	64	2.34
1970	BALTIMORE	AMERICAN	39	305	20	10	263	98	92	199	100	2.71
1971	BALTIMORE	AMERICAN	37	282	20	9	231	94	84	184	106	2.68

Year	Team	League										
1972	BALTIMORE	AMERICAN	36	274	21	10	219	73	63	184	70	2.07
1973	BALTIMORE	AMERICAN	38	296	22	9	225	86	79	153	113	2.40
1974	BALTIMORE	AMERICAN	26	179	7	12	176	78	65	84	69	3.27
1975	BALTIMORE	AMERICAN	39	323	23	11	253	87	75	193	80	2.09
1976	BALTIMORE	AMERICAN	40	315	22	13	255	101	88	159	84	2.51
1977	BALTIMORE	AMERICAN	39	319	20	11	263	106	103	193	99	2.91
1978	BALTIMORE	AMERICAN	38	296	21	12	246	94	81	138	97	2.46
1979	BALTIMORE	AMERICAN	23	156	10	6	144	66	57	67	43	3.29
1980	BALTIMORE	AMERICAN	34	224	16	10	238	108	99	109	74	3.98
1981	BALTIMORE	AMERICAN	22	127	7	8	117	60	53	35	46	3.76
1982	BALTIMORE	AMERICAN	36	227	15	5	195	85	79	103	63	3.13
1983	BALTIMORE	AMERICAN	14	76.2	5	4	86	42	36	34	19	4.23
1983	HAGERSTOWN	CAROLINA	2	13	2	0	13	6	5	11	2	3.46
1984	BALTIMORE	AMERICAN	5	17.2	0	3	22	19	18	4	17	9.17
MAJOR LEAGUE TOTALS			558	3947.1	268	152	3349	1395	1253	2212	1311	2.86

7. STEVE CARLTON

ACTIONS SPEAK LOUDER . . .

For pitcher Steve Carlton, 1972 could have been a disaster. The big (6′5″) left-hander had been traded to the Philadelphia Phillies, one of the worst teams in baseball, from one of the best teams, the St. Louis Cardinals.

Carlton had won twenty games for the Cards in 1971. He felt that he deserved a raise, a big one. Cardinals owner Gussie Busch didn't want to give it to him and decided to trade him to Philadelphia. Most people thought Carlton would be lucky to win even ten games with Philadelphia.

The Phillies *were* bad in 1972. They won only 59 games all year (each team plays 162 games). They were worse than bad; they were awful.

Except when Carlton pitched.

When Carlton pitched, the Phillies played with skill and enthusiasm. He inspired them and made them believe that they were as good as any other team.

Carlton started the season with 5 wins and a loss, but then lost 5 straight games. He then went on to win 15 straight games, giving up only 15 runs during that time. His 27 victories that year accounted for almost half of the Phillies' total wins.

"I think you could argue that Carlton's performance that year was the most dominating season any pitcher ever had," said former teammate and catcher Tim McCarver. "It is just amazing that he could have the kind of year he had with a team that was so weak."

Carlton finished the season with a 27–10 record, 310 strikeouts, and an incredible 1.96 ERA—while playing for arguably the worst team in baseball!

For accomplishing this astounding feat, Carlton was unanimously awarded the 1972 Cy Young Award, the first of a record four times he would claim the prize as the National League's top pitcher. He is the only winner of the award ever to have played for a last-place team.

Stephen Norman Carlton was born on December 22, 1944, in Miami, Florida, and grew up on the edge of the Everglades. He was always very shy and enjoyed spending time alone walking through the woods and swamps near his home.

Hunting was one of Carlton's favorite hobbies, but he was also a very good all-around athlete. His favor-

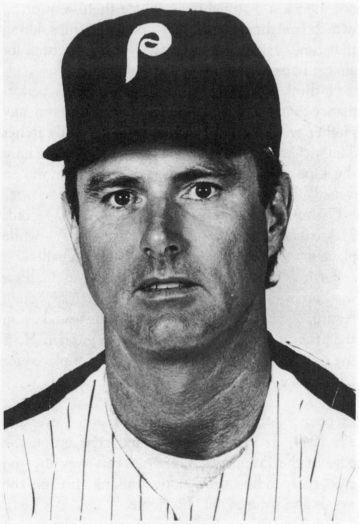

Used by permission of the National Baseball Library, Cooperstown, New York

ite sports included waterskiing, shooting pool, and golfing.

Carlton's strong left arm was noticeable at an early age. By the time he was twelve, he had developed a good curve to complement his blazing fastball. Local batters were helpless against him, and by high school it was clear he had major league potential.

In 1964, Carlton signed with St. Louis for a $5,000 bonus and was sent to Rock Hill, North Carolina, for his first experience in professional baseball. His 10–1 record and 1.03 ERA there earned him a promotion to Winnipeg, and he then moved up to the Cardinals' top minor league team, Tulsa—all in his first season!

Carlton's dominating first season earned him a place on the Cardinals in 1965. He pitched only 25 innings, though, and he began the 1966 season back in Tulsa.

In July of that year, Tulsa manager Charlie Metro approached Carlton and said, "Get ready, you're going to Cooperstown." The Cardinals were playing the American League champion Minnesota Twins in the annual Hall of Fame Game (played each year at the Baseball Hall of Fame in Cooperstown, New York), and they wanted to see how Carlton would do.

Carlton proved he belonged in the major leagues, pitching nine innings for the victory. The Cardinals were convinced, and Carlton came back to the majors for good.

Carlton had some very good years with the Cardinals. His greatest single game took place in 1969 against the New York Mets, when he set a major league record by striking out 19 batters. He struck out the side in the first two innings and headed into the ninth inning with 16 strikeouts.

With the crowd urging him on, Carlton was overpowering in the ninth. One, two, and, finally, three batters went down on strikes, and the record was Carlton's. Ironically, he lost the game, 4–3, on two two-run homers by Ron Swoboda.

Carlton had been good with the Cards, but he earned his reputation with the Phillies. He quickly became one of the league's dominant pitchers and, over time, helped the Phillies shed their losing image and become one of the league's better teams.

Following his first Cy Young Award season, Carlton began to experience arm problems. The pain was often severe, but although his arm bothered him from 1973 to 1975, he still managed to win 13, 16, and 15 games during that time.

"Lefty" (as Carlton was known around the league) was healthy in 1976, and it showed. He finished the season with 20 wins and helped the Phillies capture the National League East, their first title since they won the pennant in 1950.

Carlton gave a great deal of the credit for his success to the Phillies' strength and flexibility coach, Gus Hoefling. Under Hoefling's watchful eye, Carlton exercised harder than almost any player in baseball. He did daily martial arts exercises, ran, and lifted weights.

Carlton was totally devoted to Hoefling's workouts, which he began in 1976. On the days after he pitched, when most other pitchers rested, Carlton worked out strenuously to avoid a repeat of the injury-plagued years he had experienced from 1973 to 1975.

As a result of these workouts, Carlton was in tremendous physical condition and was one of baseball's most durable pitchers. From 1967 to 1984, he pitched 190 innings or more every year. He pitched more than 200 innings in all but two of those seasons.

The workouts also helped his strength. His fastball became even faster, and he developed a slider that was almost unhittable. His slider looked like a fastball until the last instant, when the ball would drop sharply.

In 1977, Carlton earned his second Cy Young Award. While his numbers did not match his spectacular 1972 season, they were still impressive: a 23–10 record, 198 strikeouts, and a 2.64 ERA.

Carlton was very well read, particularly in psychology and philosophy. He believed it was essential to approach every game with a positive attitude. He once tried to explain this philosophy to a group of writers, but after he struggled in a few games, some of the writers made fun of him in their stories.

As a result, Carlton made an unusual decision in 1978: He decided to quit speaking to the press. Carlton felt he had been unfairly criticized by several reporters, and he believed that he would concentrate better if he simply stopped speaking to them.

Carlton followed this policy, a rarity in professional sports, for eight years. Even though there were some media representatives he considered friends — including his old teammate, Tim McCarver, who had gone on to a broadcasting career — he didn't speak with them either.

Carlton wanted to avoid the ups and downs that come with a discussion of each win or loss. He felt it was harder to stay focused as you got older, so he didn't want distractions. The press, he clearly felt, was a distraction. He wasn't hostile or openly angry with the press. He had simply made, for him, a rational decision.

Whether this policy helped his concentration is debatable. But Carlton's concentration was legendary. He worked quickly and rarely talked to his teammates. Unlike many players, he rarely complained to umpires, for that would break his concentration. He had the ability to block out any distraction, which, combined with his belief in the power

USED BY PERMISSION OF THE NATIONAL BASEBALL LIBRARY, COOPERSTOWN, NEW YORK

of positive thinking and his strong left arm, made him a hitter's nightmare.

Carlton would do whatever was necessary to maintain his concentration. In 1980, for example, in victories over the Cubs at Wrigley Field and the Pirates at Three Rivers Stadium, he pitched with cotton stuffed in his ears to block out distracting noise.

In 1980, Carlton won a league-leading 24 games to help the Phillies become world champions. He also led the league in strikeouts (286) and innings pitched (304) and had a 2.34 ERA.

Even in the excitement of winning the World Series, Carlton was consistent in his "no press" philosophy. While journalists swarmed the clubhouse to speak with the winning players, Carlton remained in the trainer's room, a traditional off-limits area for the press.

Carlton was so consistently good in 1980 that he pitched at least 6 innings in every one of his 38 starts. Opposing teams batted only .218 against him.

The result was another Cy Young Award, Carlton's third. Three other pitchers—Sandy Koufax, Tom Seaver, and Jim Palmer—had won three Cy Young Awards, but none was as old as Carlton (thirty-five) when he won his third.

Major league players went on strike in 1981, and the strike shortened the season from 162 games to only 107. Still, Carlton managed to win 13 games while losing only 4.

"Give him a one- or two-run lead and he seldom loses," said Tim McCarver. "He has that killer instinct, particularly when he senses victory."

In 1982, Carlton started the season 0–4. He then won 23 of his next 30 decisions to finish as the major leagues' only 20-game winner. He led the National League in wins (23), shutouts (6), complete games (19), innings pitched (295), and strikeouts (286) — at the age of thirty-seven!

Carlton was a runaway winner of a record fourth Cy Young Award. Just as impressive, his latest honor occurred ten years after his first, the longest span of any multiple winner.

A game against San Diego that season was typical of Carlton's dominance. San Diego batters singled on Carlton's first three pitches, scoring once. Carlton remained calm, though, and promptly picked off the runner on first. He then struck out the next two batters to escape from trouble and went on to win the game, 3–1.

Carlton was only an average pitcher in 1983. His record slipped to 15–16, although he did manage to lead the league in strikeouts for the fifth time. More important, he won his three hundredth game, assuring him a place in the Hall of Fame.

Age began to take a toll in 1984. Although he won 13 games, Carlton pitched his fewest innings (not counting the strike season) since 1967. He won only one game in 1985, and a rotator cuff injury to his shoulder drove him to the disabled list for the first time in his career.

"Like a lot of great athletes, Carlton felt almost superhuman," said Tim McCarver, explaining why Carlton didn't retire sooner. "A lot of what made him great was what made him hang on at the end of his career."

Carlton didn't care about making a graceful exit from baseball. He wanted to surpass Warren Spahn (who had 363 career victories) as the winningest left-hander in baseball history.

But Carlton's skills were fading fast. After struggling to a 4–8 record in the first two months of 1986, he was released by the Phillies. He then pitched a month with the San Francisco Giants and two months with the Chicago White Sox.

Carlton shocked the baseball world when, after signing with the Giants, he gave his first interview in eight years. During the interview, he stated his desire to pitch until he was fifty years old.

But fifty was asking too much of his left arm. After winning only 6 games while losing 14 in 1987 (for the Cleveland Indians and the Minnesota Twins) and appearing in only 4 games early in the 1988 season, Carlton finally retired.

He won 329 games in his career, second only to Spahn among left-handers. His 4,136 career strikeouts trailed only Nolan Ryan. He won 20 games six times, and led the league in strikeouts five times and in wins four times. Carlton also had 18 consecutive years of 100 or more strikeouts.

But his greatest achievement is undoubtedly his four Cy Young Awards, more than any other player in history.

Carlton avoided the press for most of his career, but it didn't really matter. What he did on the field spoke for itself.

STEVE CARLTON—CAREER STATISTICS

YEAR	CLUB	LEAGUE	G	IP	W	L	H	R	ER	SO	BB	ERA
1964	ROCK HILL	W. CAROLINAS	11	79	10	1	39	17	9	91	36	1.03
1964	WINNIPEG	NORTHERN	12	75	4	4	63	40	28	79	48	3.36
1964	TULSA	TEXAS	4	24	1	1	16	13	7	21	18	2.63
1965	ST. LOUIS	NATIONAL	15	25	0	0	27	7	7	21	8	2.52
1966	TULSA	P.C.	19	128	9	5	110	65	51	108	54	3.59
1966	ST. LOUIS	NATIONAL	9	52	3	3	56	22	18	25	18	3.12
1967	ST. LOUIS	NATIONAL	30	193	14	9	173	71	64	168	62	2.98
1968	ST. LOUIS	NATIONAL	34	232	13	11	214	87	77	162	61	2.99
1969	ST. LOUIS	NATIONAL	31	236	17	11	185	66	57	210	93	2.17
1970	ST. LOUIS	NATIONAL	34	254	10	19	239	123	105	193	109	3.72
1971	ST. LOUIS	NATIONAL	37	273	20	9	275	120	108	172	98	3.56
1972	PHILADELPHIA	NATIONAL	41	346	27	10	257	84	76	310	87	1.98
1973	PHILADELPHIA	NATIONAL	40	293	13	20	293	146	127	223	113	3.90
1974	PHILADELPHIA	NATIONAL	39	291	16	13	249	118	104	240	136	3.22

Year	Team	League										ERA
1975	PHILADELPHIA	NATIONAL	37	255	15	14	217	116	101	192	104	3.56
1976	PHILADELPHIA	NATIONAL	35	253	20	7	224	94	88	195	72	3.13
1977	PHILADELPHIA	NATIONAL	36	283	23	10	229	99	83	198	89	2.64
1978	PHILADELPHIA	NATIONAL	34	247	16	13	228	91	78	161	63	2.84
1979	PHILADELPHIA	NATIONAL	35	251	18	11	202	112	101	213	89	3.62
1980	PHILADELPHIA	NATIONAL	38	304	24	9	243	87	79	286	90	2.34
1981	PHILADELPHIA	NATIONAL	24	190	13	4	152	59	51	179	62	2.42
1982	PHILADELPHIA	NATIONAL	38	295.2	23	11	253	114	102	286	86	3.10
1983	PHILADELPHIA	NATIONAL	37	283.2	15	16	277	117	98	275	84	3.11
1984	PHILADELPHIA	NATIONAL	33	229	13	7	214	104	91	163	79	3.58
1985	PHILADELPHIA	NATIONAL	16	92	1	8	84	43	34	48	53	3.33
1986	PHILADELPHIA-SAN FRANCISCO	NATIONAL	22	113	5	11	138	90	74	80	61	5.89
1986	CHICAGO	AMERICAN	10	63.1	4	3	58	30	26	40	25	3.69
1987	CLEVELAND-MINNESOTA	AMERICAN	32	152	6	14	165	111	97	91	86	5.74
1988	MINNESOTA	AMERICAN	4	9.2	0	1	20	19	18	5	5	16.76
MAJOR LEAGUE TOTALS (25 YEARS)			**741**	**5216.2**	**329**	**244**	**4672**	**2130**	**1864**	**4136**	**1833**	**3.22**

8. FERNANDO VALENZUELA

THE "FEVER" SPREADS

In 1981, a plump left-handed pitcher from Mexico exploded onto the American baseball scene. His name was Fernando Valenzuela and he played for the Los Angeles Dodgers. He had pitched only a few innings for the Dodgers at the end of the 1980 season, and so 1981 was still considered his rookie year.

And what a rookie year it was.

It began on Opening Day, when the Dodgers asked the twenty-year-old to pitch in place of injured veteran Jerry Reuss. It is a lot to ask a rookie to pitch the first game of the season. Opening Day is much more exciting and tense than almost any other regular-season game, and even established veterans are nervous as the season begins.

But the pressure didn't seem to bother Valenzuela at all. Or if it did, he didn't show it. Pitching with the confidence and composure of a ten-year veteran, he shut out the Houston Astros on five hits, striking out five batters and walking only two.

When reporters tried to talk to Valenzuela after the game, they ran into one problem: Valenzuela didn't speak English.

Fernando Anguamea Valenzuela was born on November 1, 1960, in a small farming community on the west coast of Mexico. He was the youngest of twelve children and had six brothers and five sisters. The Valenzuela family was very poor. Fernando's father grew beans and corn on a small, half-acre farm. The Valenzuela sons worked on larger ranches in the afternoons to help make extra money for the family.

Like many Mexican youngsters, Valenzuela was attracted to baseball and played whenever he had the chance. It soon became apparent that he had a natural feel for the game. After only one year in high school, he signed a contract to play professionally in Mexico.

In the summer of 1978, Los Angeles Dodgers scout Mike Brito was in Mexico to look at a talented shortstop. Valenzuela happened to be pitching that night against the shortstop's team, and Brito saw the seventeen-year-old dominate the game with 12 strikeouts (including a strikeout of the shortstop Brito had come to see).

Brito was impressed with Valenzuela and told the Dodgers to keep an eye on this promising left-hander. The Dodgers went to Mexico to see Valen-

USED BY PERMISSION OF THE NATIONAL BASEBALL LIBRARY, COOPERSTOWN,
NEW YORK

zuela play again the next year, and they decided to offer him a contract with their team.

But the Dodgers weren't the only team interested in Valenzuela. The Yankees also wanted him, and a bidding war was soon under way.

The Dodgers won that fight with an offer of $120,000 and bought out Valenzuela's existing contract with Puebla of the Mexican Center League. The future star was sent to Lodi, a Class A California League team, for his first professional experience in the United States.

Valenzuela gave up a mere 3 earned runs in 24 innings pitched at Lodi, relying on the fastball and curve that the Dodgers had first noticed in Mexico. But Dodger management felt Valenzuela needed to develop another pitch to be successful in the major leagues, and they asked him to spend the winter at the Arizona Instructional League.

Dodger relief pitcher Bobby Castillo, assisted by pitching coach Ron Perranoski, began teaching Valenzuela the screwball. The screwball, which breaks in the opposite direction of a curve, is one of the most difficult pitches to master. The most famous screwball pitcher of all time, Hall of Famer Carl Hubbell, spent seven years learning how to control the pitch.

But Valenzuela was different. He seemed comfortable with the new pitch almost immediately. "He picked it up right away!" marveled Perranoski. Soon

Valenzuela was using his screwball 60 to 70 percent of the time.

Valenzuela began 1980 with the Dodgers' minor league team in San Antonio. He won 13 games and lost 9 before the Dodgers called him up to the major leagues, but the numbers don't tell the whole story. Valenzuela spent the first part of the year learning how to use the screwball in actual games. As the nineteen-year-old became more comfortable with the screwball, his effectiveness as a pitcher improved dramatically.

In the last six weeks at San Antonio, Valenzuela's record was 7–0. "He may not speak good English," said Ducky LeJohn, the San Antonio manager, "but he speaks pretty good baseball." More impressive than his win-loss record was the fact that he had not given up *a single earned run in 35 innings of pitching.*

The Dodgers were impressed. They were in the middle of a pennant race and needed some pitching help. Valenzuela was called up to Los Angeles for the last month of the season.

A pennant race is a pressure-filled situation for everyone, even the most experienced veterans. Only a handful of players can successfully launch their big league careers in the middle of such tension.

Valenzuela was one of those players. He seemed totally unaffected by the drama going on around him. When he was called upon to pitch, he responded with the same confidence and authority he had shown since he first began pitching in Mexico.

The Dodgers used him as a relief pitcher in 1980, and Valenzuela pitched 17⅔ innings before the season ended. No one could have asked for better results. He won two games for the Dodgers, lost none, did not give up a single earned run, and helped Los Angeles tie the Houston Astros for the National League West title.

In the one-game playoff with Houston, Valenzuela pitched two more scoreless innings. Although Los Angeles lost the game, Valenzuela had clearly shown he was ready for big league competition.

"Fernando Fever," as it was called, struck with full force in 1981. It began in Los Angeles, where the city's more than 2 million Hispanics quickly claimed Valenzuela as one of their own. But the fever spread to other big-league cities and, soon, to baseball fans all across the United States.

Following his Opening Day shutout of Houston — the same team he had faced in the playoffs in 1980 — Valenzuela beat the San Francisco Giants, 7–1, while striking out 10 batters. His next victim was San Diego, whom he shut out, 2–0, on 5 hits. He had 10 strikeouts in that game and no walks.

Valenzuela's winning streak continued in his next game, another matchup with Houston. Valenzuela scattered 7 hits and struck out 11 in a 1–0 win over the Astros. To top it off, he had 2 hits in 3 at bats and drove in the game's only run.

After his first four major league starts, Valenzuela's record was 4–0. He had pitched 4 complete games and had 3 shutouts. His ERA was a remarkable 0.25. Everywhere the Dodgers played, huge crowds flocked to see this unusual star. The crowds also included an unusually large number of media. Representatives from newspapers, magazines, television programs, and radio shows all wanted to talk with Valenzuela.

Although he was beginning to learn a few words, Valenzuela's English was very limited. He was assisted by an interpreter in all postgame interviews.

One of Valenzuela's most appealing characteristics was his physical appearance. He looked much heavier than the 200 pounds he carried on his 5'11" frame. The average fan could easily identify with this seemingly out-of-shape player. But looks can be deceiving. Valenzuela was actually in great shape. He ran three miles a day, and his training showed in his pitching.

Valenzuela went on to win his first eight games in the strike-shortened 1981 season. He finished the year with 11 complete games (tops in the National League), 192 innings pitched, and 8 shutouts (an N.L. rookie record). He struck out 180 batters, becoming the first rookie to lead the National League in this category. He also posted a 2.48 ERA and fin-

Used by permission of the National Baseball Library, Cooperstown, New York

ished the season with 13 wins, second only to Tom Seaver's 14. He even batted .250, an unusually high batting average for a pitcher.

Valenzuela's dominance continued in the playoffs and World Series, where he won three games while losing only one. Highlighting his postseason performance was Game 3 of the World Series against the New York Yankees. Valenzuela gave up 6 hits, 4 walks, and 4 runs in the first three innings and looked as if he would be beaten badly.

But Dodgers manager Tommy Lasorda had faith in his young star and kept him in the game. Valenzuela allowed only six more base runners for the rest of the game, and the Dodgers won 5–4.

Everyone expected Valenzuela to win the Rookie of the Year Award that year, which he did, easily. He also captured the Cy Young Award, edging out Seaver for the honor. He became the first player to win the Rookie of the Year and the Cy Young awards in the same season.

The charismatic left-hander was almost as successful in 1982. He was second in the National League in wins (19) and third in ERA (2.87), and finished third in the Cy Young voting, won for an unprecedented fourth time by Philadelphia's Steve Carlton.

Valenzuela's all-around athletic ability was put to good use that year in a 21-inning game in Chicago. As the extraordinarily long game continued, both teams found themselves running out of players. Valenzuela played both right field and left field as the Dodgers finally won the marathon game, 2–1.

Valenzuela set a major league record in 1985 when he began the season without allowing an earned run in his first 41 innings. He finished the year with 17 wins.

He was even better in 1986. He led the National League with a career-high 21 wins, and his 20 complete games (also an N.L. best) were the most by a National League pitcher since Atlanta's Phil Niekro had 23 in 1979. He also had a career-high 242 strikeouts.

At the 1986 All-Star Game at the Houston Astrodome, Valenzuela tied Carl Hubbell's All-Star Game record of five consecutive strikeouts. In the fourth inning, he struck out Don Mattingly, Cal Ripken, and Jesse Barfield. He also fanned the first two batters in the fifth inning, Lou Whitaker and Ted Higuera.

Although Valenzuela did not win the 1986 Cy Young Award, he finished second in the voting to Houston's Mike Scott. Valenzuela did win one award that year, a Gold Glove for his outstanding fielding.

From 1987 to 1990, bothered by a series of nagging injuries and hampered by some weak Dodger teams, Valenzuela struggled to regain the form that had made him one of the league's most dominant pitchers earlier in the decade. The best he could do, though, was win as many games as he lost.

But on June 29, 1990, none of that mattered. Pitching against the St. Louis Cardinals, Valenzuela threw a no-hitter as the Dodgers won, 6–0. He got the final outs by forcing former teammate Pedro Guerrero to hit into a game-ending double play.

Valenzuela and the Dodgers parted company in the spring of 1991 as Los Angeles released its former star pitcher. Valenzuela is prominently featured on many of the Dodgers' all-time lists. His 1,759 strikeouts rank him fifth among Dodgers and, among lefthanders, second only to Sandy Koufax. His 141 wins rank eighth in Dodger history, and his 29 shutouts rank fifth.

He led the Dodgers in complete games for seven consecutive years ('81–'87). He led the team in innings pitched and strikeouts for six consecutive years ('81–'86). Between 1981 and 1987 he won 97 games, second only to Detroit's Jack Morris among major league pitchers.

Following his release by the Dodgers, the California Angels signed Valenzuela to a contract. He was defeated in both of the two games he started for California, and was released by the Angels shortly thereafter. His professional baseball career, at least in America, seemed over.

The Mexican League welcomed Valenzuela back, and he won ten games in the league in 1992. In 1993, he was offered a tryout with the American League's Baltimore Orioles. Although most doubted that he still possessed the talent to pitch at the major league level, he won a position on Baltimore's pitch-ing staff and played an important role as the Orioles contended for the American League East title.

The personable pitcher who had captivated the sports world in 1981 showed that he still had a few surprises left.

FERNANDO VALENZUELA—CAREER STATISTICS

YEAR	CLUB	LEAGUE	G	IP	W	L	H	R	ER	SO	BB	ERA
1978	GUANAJUATO		16	93.0	5	6	88	46	23	91	46	2.23
1979	YUCATAN-1		26	181.0	10	12	157	68	50	141	70	2.49
	LODI		3	24.0	1	2	21	10	3	18	3	1.13
1980	SAN ANTONIO		27	174.0	13	9	156	70	60	162	70	3.10
	LOS ANGELES	NATIONAL	10	18.0	2	0	8	2	0	16	5	0.00
1981	LOS ANGELES	NATIONAL	25	192.0	13	7	140	55	53	180	61	2.48
1982	LOS ANGELES	NATIONAL	37	285.0	19	13	247	105	91	199	83	2.87
1983	LOS ANGELES	NATIONAL	35	257.0	15	10	245	122	107	189	99	3.75
1984	LOS ANGELES	NATIONAL	34	261.0	12	17	218	109	88	240	106	3.03

Year	Team	League	G	IP	W	L	H	R	ER	SO	BB	ERA
1985	Los Angeles	National	35	272.1	17	10	211	92	74	208	101	2.45
1986	Los Angeles	National	34	269.1	21	11	226	104	94	242	85	3.14
1987	Los Angeles	National	34	251.0	14	14	254	120	111	190	124	3.98
1988	Los Angeles	National	23	142.1	5	8	142	71	67	64	76	4.24
1989	Los Angeles	National	31	196.2	10	13	185	89	75	116	98	3.43
1990	Los Angeles	National	33	204.0	13	13	223	112	104	115	77	4.59
1991	Palm Springs		1	4.0	0	0	4	1	0	2	3	0.00
	Midland		4	23.0	3	1	18	5	5	17	6	1.96
	Edmonton		7	36.2	3	3	48	34	29	36	17	7.12
	California		2	6.2	0	2	14	10	9	5	3	12.15
1992	Jalisco		22	156.0	10	9	154	81	67	98	51	3.86
1993	Baltimore	American	32	178.2	8	10	179	104	98	78	79	4.94
MAJOR LEAGUE TOTALS			365	2534.0	149	128	2292	1095	971	1842	997	**3.45**

9. DWIGHT GOODEN

THE YOUNGEST CY YOUNG AWARD WINNER

Dwight Eugene Gooden was only nineteen years old when he became a star pitcher for the New York Mets. It is rare to find a player that young who can even *make* a major league team, but it is rarer still to find someone who is a star at that age.

Domination was what "Doc" Gooden was all about. He threw a blazing fastball—one of the game's hardest—that made him one of the most overpowering pitchers in the game.

Gooden's second most effective pitch was a hard, overhand curveball. It looked almost exactly like his fastball, until the batter started to swing. Then the ball quickly dropped, leaving the batter confused and frustrated.

To make matters worse for batters, Gooden was one of the best control pitchers in the game. He could throw the ball almost exactly where he wanted it to go, and he rarely walked a batter.

The entire country seemed to embrace him as his 1984 rookie season progressed. As he struck out batter after batter, the fans at the Mets' Shea Stadium started a "K Corner." (A "K" is baseball shorthand for a strikeout.) The fans kept track of each Gooden strikeout by hanging "K" signs on the railings of the stadium.

They had a lot to keep track of in 1984. Not only did Gooden win 17 games in his first year, the nineteen-year-old also led the majors in strikeouts with 276 in only 218 innings pitched. He averaged 11.39 strikeouts per 9 innings pitched, shattering Cleveland Indian pitcher Sam McDowell's record.

By the end of the year, Gooden was being compared with Hall of Fame pitcher Bob Feller, who started in major league baseball at age seventeen in 1936. Feller was one of the game's best strikeout pitchers and, at age nineteen, struck out 240 batters while also winning 17 games. But Feller walked 208 batters that year; Gooden walked only 73.

That summer, Gooden became the youngest player ever to appear in the All-Star Game. He struck out the side in the first inning he pitched, giving American League batters a taste of what National League batters had been experiencing since the beginning of the year.

"I wasn't even supposed to make the team that year," said Gooden. "Davey Johnson [the Mets' manager] brought me to spring training because I had pitched for him in the AAA [minor league] playoffs the previous year. I expected to pitch one more season of minor league ball, but Tom Seaver had gone to the White Sox and I pitched well in spring training. But I couldn't believe it when I found myself in the All-Star Game.

"Gary Carter was catching and he was pumping his fist at me, saying, 'Let's go!' I struck out the first three batters I faced. That's something I'll never forget."

As Gooden ran off the mound at the end of the inning, Carter ran up to him. "I wish we could do that for a whole season," Carter said. At the end of the 1984 season, Carter was granted his wish. He was traded to the Mets and would witness firsthand one of the most dominating seasons in major league history.

Gooden grew up in Tampa, Florida. His father, Dan Gooden, coached a local semipro team, the Tampa Dodgers. Dan took his son to games at an early age, when Gooden was so small he could only roll a baseball along the ground.

As Gooden grew older, baseball became an even greater influence in his life. While his friends played a variety of sports, Gooden concentrated almost exclusively on baseball.

"Baseball was just in my blood, mostly because of my father," said Gooden. "It was always the number-

COURTESY OF THE NEW YORK METS

one thing. Even if it was football season, if there was one guy who wanted to play catch, I'd play catch with that one guy."

By the time Gooden was at Hillsborough High School, he was one of the area's best pitchers. Next to his father, Gooden believes that high school coach Billy Reed had the greatest influence on his development.

"Coach Reed treated everybody the same," said Gooden. "He didn't care about your athletic ability as much as he did about what kind of person you were. He also helped the guys that were good enough to be drafted by preparing them for the next level of competition."

Gooden was definitely good enough to be drafted, though it took a bit of luck to speed the process. One day several baseball scouts came to see another Hillsborough High pitcher. That pitcher was wild, though, and was replaced by Gooden. The scouts started to leave the game, but quickly returned when they heard Gooden's mighty fastball cracking into the catcher's mitt.

In the 1982 draft, Gooden was selected by the Mets, the fifth player taken in the first round. He won five games and lost four at Kingsport, the Mets' Class A team, as he adapted to professional baseball. In 1983, he went 19–4 with 300 strikeouts at Lynchburg (Virginia) in the Carolina League. The following spring, he became a Met.

Not only did Gooden easily win the Rookie of the Year Award in 1984, he was second in the Cy Young Award voting, an amazing feat for a rookie. He gives much of the credit for his success to his father, whom he called after every game.

"I called him a lot back then," said Gooden. "He was like my assistant pitching coach. He always gave me support, but he was always trying to help me get better, too. Even if I pitched a one-to-nothing shut-out, he'd say, 'That was a good game, but you should have pitched this hitter that way, and done such and such in a certain situation.' He made sure I didn't relax too much after I pitched, that I kept working and learning."

Gooden was practically unbeatable in 1985. He led the major leagues with 24 wins while losing only 4, a winning percentage of .857. His 268 strikeouts and 1.53 ERA also led the majors, making him the first player to lead in all three categories since Sandy Koufax accomplished the feat in 1966.

Late that summer, Gooden, twenty, became the youngest 20-game winner in major league baseball history. Once again the comparison was to Bob Feller, as Gooden beat Feller's old record by twenty-seven days.

Gooden's incredible season—at one point, he won 14 games in a row—made him a hero to millions. He appeared on the covers of *Sports Illustrated*, *Time*, and *New York* magazines. He could do no wrong, it seemed, and the batters could do nothing right.

"You just get into a zone where everything is working," said Gooden. "I probably appreciate it more now than I did at the time. I felt like I only needed one or two runs each game, that was enough.

"I just focused on the hitter. Guys were stealing bases on me left and right, but it didn't matter, because I knew I was going to get the batter out. I couldn't wait for each start, couldn't wait to get back on the mound and face that next batter.

"I remember one game in Dodger Stadium, where I've had a lot of success. I was pitching against Fernando Valenzuela, who also had a great year.

"We both pitched nine innings of shutout ball. I remember that the Dodgers had the bases loaded in the ninth inning, with nobody out. Davey Johnson came out to the mound and said, 'They're going to send up three left-handed batters against you. I think I'm going to bring in Jesse Orosco.'

"I said, 'No way, you've got to give me a chance to get out of this.' I ended up getting the first guy to pop up, then I struck out the next two batters to end the inning. I gave Davey a little wink when I got back to the dugout, just to let him know I had everything under control."

Gooden had the entire season under control. At the end of the year, the Baseball Writers Association of America unanimously selected him as the Cy Young Award winner. Gooden, still only twenty, became the youngest player to win the Cy Young.

Gooden picked up other honors following his amazing 1985 season. He showed his all-around athletic ability by capturing the National League Silver Bat Award as the league's top-hitting pitcher. More important, the Associated Press named him its Male Athlete of the Year, choosing him over male athletes in every sport, not just baseball.

Gooden's on-the-field success and off-the-field politeness made him a fan favorite. While it would have been easy to become conceited and arrogant, Gooden remained as good-natured as he had always been. The credit for that, he says, goes to Coach Billy Reed and, especially, to his parents.

"Billy Reed and my parents kept me grounded," he said. "My parents taught me to just be yourself, whether you are a ballplayer, a doctor, or anything else. Don't forget where you were before you became a star.

"Coach Reed taught all of his players that being a better athlete doesn't make you a better person. My parents reinforced that lesson at home, and it's something I've never forgotten."

With three games remaining in the 1985 season, the Mets trailed the St. Louis Cardinals by three games. By chance, their remaining games were with the Cardinals. If they won all three, there would be a one-game playoff for the National League East title.

The Mets won the first game behind the pitching of Ron Darling, and trailed by only two games. In the second game, Gooden was on the mound.

"We were leading, though I had been struggling most of the game," said Gooden. "The Cardinals were down to their last batter, Tommy Herr, but a base hit could win the game for them. Herr hit a line drive, but it was caught and we won the game. After winning two straight, we were confident that we would win the final game and force the playoff."

But the Mets lost that final game, giving St. Louis the championship. Still, New York—led by Gooden's incredible individual effort—had had a great season. The team was supremely confident as it entered the 1986 season.

Once again, Gooden was the ace of the pitching staff. Although no longer unbeatable, he still won 17 games while striking out 200 batters, his third consecutive season with 200 or more strikeouts.

The Mets, though, *were* unbeatable. Or so it seemed to the rest of the National League, as New York won 108 games while winning its division by 21½ games.

The Mets knocked off the Houston Astros in the playoffs and then won a seven-game World Series against the Boston Red Sox. The sixth game of that

Series featured a New York tenth-inning comeback that dramatically ended when Boston first baseman Bill Buckner missed an easy ground ball that would have resulted in an out and a Series win for the Red Sox.

Following that championship season, several million New Yorkers turned out for the ticker-tape parade honoring the Mets. Gooden was noticeably absent, and claimed he had overslept.

Later that winter, Gooden and several of his friends were stopped by the Tampa police for possible traffic violations. A fight broke out, and Gooden was arrested.

Mets fans were surprised and saddened by the news. Gooden had always been a fan favorite, and was known for his politeness and cheery disposition. What could possibly explain this behavior?

The answer came in April of 1987, just prior to the beginning of the new season. Gooden checked himself into the Smithers Alcoholism and Drug Treatment Center in New York City. The problem: cocaine.

Gooden overcame his drug problem and returned to baseball in June of that year. He was apologetic for his behavior and for letting the Mets and the fans down. Players and fans alike welcomed him back, not condoning his behavior but forgiving him for it.

Despite playing only a little more than half the

year, Gooden still won 15 games. In a full season in 1988, he won 18 more. Slowly he was learning that he could be a very good major league pitcher, even if he never duplicated 1985.

"For a few seasons after '85, I expected to do the same thing: win twenty-four or twenty-five games while leading the league in strikeouts," said Gooden. "I was always trying to get ten strikeouts instead of focusing on my pitching. Then I began to realize that I could be a good pitcher and put up some very good numbers without having to match '85."

Gooden continued to pitch consistently well. Through the 1992 season, he had won 142 games while losing only 66. His career winning percentage of .683 was the best in National League history and fourth best of all-time.

More important, Gooden had recaptured the joy of playing baseball. Gone was the pressure to repeat that wondrous '85 season. Instead, he simply concentrated on each game, determined to do the best he could.

A baseball hero had grown up.

DWIGHT GOODEN — CAREER STATISTICS

YEAR	CLUB	LEAGUE	G	IP	W	L	H	R	ER	SO	BB	ERA
1982	KINGSPORT	A	9	66.0	5	4	53	34	18	66	25	2.47
	LITTLE FALLS	A	2	13.0	0	1	11	6	6	18	3	4.15
1983	LYNCHBURG	A	27	191.0	*19	4	121	58	53	*300	112	*2.50
1984	NEW YORK	NATIONAL	31	218.0	17	9	161	72	63	*276	73	2.60
1985	NEW YORK	NATIONAL	35	276.2	*24	4	198	51	47	*268	69	*1.53
1986	NEW YORK	NATIONAL	33	250.0	17	6	197	92	79	200	80	2.84
1987	TIDEWATER	AAA#	4	22.0	3	0	20	7	5	24	9	2.05
	LYNCHBURG	A#	1	4.0	0	0	2	0	0	3	2	0.00

1987	NEW YORK	NATIONAL	25	179.2	15	7	162	68	64	148	53	3.21
1988	NEW YORK	NATIONAL	34	248.1	18	9	242	98	88	175	57	3.19
1989	NEW YORK	NATIONAL	19	118.1	9	4	93	42	38	101	47	2.89
1990	NEW YORK	NATIONAL	34	232.2	19	7	229	106	99	223	70	3.83
1991	NEW YORK	NATIONAL	27	190.0	13	7	185	80	76	150	56	3.60
1992	NEW YORK	NATIONAL	31	206.0	10	13	197	93	84	145	70	3.67
1993	NEW YORK	NATIONAL	29	208.2	12	15	188	89	80	149	61	3.45
MINOR LEAGUE TOTALS			**43**	**296.0**	**27**	**9**	**207**	**105**	**82**	**411**	**151**	**2.49**
MAJOR LEAGUE TOTALS			**298**	**2127.2**	**154**	**81**	**1852**	**791**	**718**	**1835**	**636**	**3.04**

* LED LEAGUE   # REHAB ASSIGNMENT

10. ROGER CLEMENS

THE ROCKET TAKES OFF

As twenty-three-year-old Boston Red Sox pitcher Roger "Rocket" Clemens took the mound on April 29, 1986, the 13,414 fans at Fenway Park had no reason to expect anything unusual to happen. The opposition, the lowly Seattle Mariners, excited no one. In fact, given the opportunity, most of the fans would have been at the Boston Celtics' playoff game on the other side of town.

All in all, it promised to be just another evening of baseball.

Baseball is a funny game, though. Amid all the games—each team plays 162—great things do happen. And no one can predict when or where they will occur.

Clemens struck out the side in the first inning, all on 3–2 fastballs, the first of three times he would strike out the side that night. Red Sox fans listening to the Celtics game on their radios began to pay a little more attention to the action in front of them.

Clemens struck out two more Mariners in the second inning and one in the third. In the fourth inning, Red Sox first baseman Don Baylor inadvertently helped Clemens by dropping Gordon Thomas's foul pop-up. Clemens then struck out Thomas for his third strikeout of the inning and his ninth of the game.

Relying almost exclusively on fastballs, the big (6'4", 215 pounds) right-hander struck out the side again in the fifth. He struck out the first two batters in the sixth inning, tying the league record of 8 consecutive strikeouts. He now had 14 strikeouts for the game, and the fans were cheering wildly with every pitch he made.

Clemens was one of the hardest throwers in baseball, and his fastball was practically untouchable that night. Radar clocked him between 95 and 97 mph all night, and the Mariners looked like Little Leaguers facing a high school star.

Mariners Phil Bradley and Ken Phelps went down on fastballs in the seventh inning, giving Clemens 16 strikeouts for the game. Gordon Thomas did manage to hit a solo home run, Seattle's second hit of the entire game.

Clemens picked up his seventeenth and eighteenth strikeouts in the eighth inning. In the bottom of the eighth inning, teammate Al Nipper informed him that he was only one strikeout away from tying the major league record.

Only three other pitchers had ever struck out 19 batters in a nine-inning game. In 1969, Steve Carlton struck out 19 for the St. Louis Cardinals in a 4–3 loss to the New York Mets. The following year, the Mets' Tom Seaver struck out 19 San Diego Padres. Clemens's idol, Nolan Ryan, fanned 19 in 1974 as his California Angels defeated the Red Sox.

Mariner shortstop Spike Owen was the first batter to face Clemens in the ninth. Clemens struck him out on a 1–2 fastball, and the crowd roared as the scoreboard message was posted: "Roger Clemens Has Tied the Major League Record for Strikeouts in a 9-Inning Game With 19."

Now players from both teams were standing in their dugouts, wondering if they were about to witness a baseball first. Even major league baseball players—who witness incredible athletic feats on a regular basis—become fans during historic moments. Of course, the fans were standing too, applauding every pitch.

Mariner left-fielder Phil Bradley slowly approached the plate. He had already struck out three times, and he was determined not to become a part of baseball history.

But Clemens had other ideas. The crowd roared as a 2–2 fastball sent Bradley back to the dugout for Clemens's twentieth strikeout of the game. The final batter, Ken Phelps, grounded out to give Clemens a 3–1, three-hit victory.

Clemens's cap, spikes, glove, and the record-setting baseball were immediately sent to the Baseball Hall of Fame in Cooperstown, New York. Boston manager John McNamara, who had witnessed perfect games by Catfish Hunter and Mike Witt, called Clemens's effort "the most amazing pitching performance I've ever seen."

Another amazing feat was that Clemens did not walk a single batter the entire evening, demonstrating a perfect combination of power and control. But perhaps the most amazing feat was that Clemens was pitching at all, eight months after a shoulder operation had threatened to end his career.

William Roger Clemens was born on August 4, 1962, in Dayton, Ohio. As a boy he spent endless hours in front of a mirror perfecting his pitching motion.

His family moved to Houston, Texas, and Clemens used to go to the Astrodome to watch Nolan Ryan throw his blazing fastball for the Astros. He was inspired by Ryan and determined to become the same type of pitcher.

Clemens pitched for his high school and American Legion teams, but his fastball never went much above the 80-mph mark. Still, he was good enough to lead his American Legion team to the Texas state championship in 1979.

The Minnesota Twins drafted Clemens out of high

COURTESY OF THE BOSTON RED SOX

school, but he chose to continue his education at San Jacinto Junior College. After one year at San Jacinto, he was offered a baseball scholarship to the University of Texas.

At the same time, though, he had a tryout with the New York Mets. When he failed to impress the Mets, he decided to attend Texas.

He went on to star for the Longhorns and, in 1983, he led them to the College World Series. Clemens was the winning pitcher as Texas beat Alabama, 4–3, for the NCAA title. He then went home and waited for the major league draft.

The Red Sox made Clemens their first pick in the draft, and Clemens headed to Winter Haven, Florida, the Sox's Class A minor league team. In four starts, he recorded 36 strikeouts without walking a single batter, while posting a 3–1 record.

From Winter Haven, Clemens moved to the Double A level in New Britain, Connecticut. His 4–1 record and 1.38 ERA earned him a promotion to Pawtucket at the Triple A level in 1984.

Although his record was only 2–3 in his short time there, his strikeout ability (50 in 46 innings) and 1.93 ERA showed the Red Sox he had the right stuff. They called him up to the big leagues in May of 1984.

Clemens proved immediately that he was ready for major league competition. He won nine games in three and a half months, and people began to compare him to Doc Gooden, the New York Mets' young star pitcher. Unfortunately, a strained forearm prevented him from pitching the last month of the season.

Injuries continued to be a problem for Clemens in 1985. He was bothered by weakness in his shoulder, and continued to pitch even without his strong fastball. Finally, though, the pain became too much, and late in the summer he agreed to have shoulder surgery.

The operation was a success, and Clemens faithfully followed his rehabilitation schedule. But in his first three spring training appearances in 1986, opposing batters hit him hard.

The problem was that Clemens had lost confidence in his trademark fastball. Red Sox pitching coach Bill Fischer approached Clemens and asked him if he was avoiding using his best pitch. "How hard do you think you are throwing?" the coach asked.

Clemens thought his fastball was only going around 84 mph. Fischer gave him the radar-gun printout, which showed his fastball was constantly hitting 93 mph.

As his confidence improved, Clemens began to use his fastball more. It took an April 22 appearance against the Detroit Tigers, however, before he felt completely confident again. He struck out 10 batters in 6⅔ innings, and knew for certain that he had overcome any effects of his shoulder surgery.

Clemens was unbeatable for the first half of the season, winning his first 14 decisions, the fifth-best start in major league history. By the All-Star Game, his record was 15–2. He was the starting pitcher for the American League All-Stars and was named the game's Most Valuable Player.

He finished the year with a 24–4 record, leading the league in wins, winning percentage (.857), and ERA (2.48), while striking out 238 batters.

In leading the Sox to the division title, Clemens showed a maturity far beyond someone with less than three years of major league experience. Pitching like a seasoned veteran, he won fourteen of his games after Boston defeats, ensuring that the Red Sox did not suffer any prolonged losing streaks.

The Red Sox won the '86 American League Championship series after trailing the California Angels three games to one. Their opponents in the World Series were the New York Mets.

In Game 2, Clemens squared off against Mets ace Doc Gooden. But it was not Gooden's day, and Clemens and the Sox were easy 9–3 winners.

With the Sox leading three games to two, Clemens started Game 6. The Red Sox were leading, 3–2, in the eighth inning when Clemens had to leave the game with a blister on his pitching hand. It soon became one of the most painful blisters in Red Sox history.

The Mets, trailing 5–3, were down to their last strike when they staged a most improbable rally. They finally won the game when an easy ground ball trickled through the legs of Red Sox first baseman Bill Buckner. The Sox went on to lose Game 7 and the World Series.

Clemens was an easy winner of the 1986 Cy Young Award, and his extraordinary season also enabled him to capture Most Valuable Player honors. It was the first time a player had won the Cy Young, MVP, and All-Star Game MVP in the same season.

Clemens picked up a host of other awards, including the *Sporting News* Player of the Year. Clemens, Sandy Koufax (in 1963), and Denny McLain (in 1968) are the only pitchers to win the MVP, Cy Young, and *Sporting News* Player of the Year honors in the same season.

In 1987, Clemens walked out of spring training in a dispute over his contract. The issue was soon resolved, but the disruption seemed to affect him at the beginning of the season. He struggled to a 4–6 record in his first ten decisions.

The 1987 season was also particularly challenging for Clemens because he was constantly reminded of how difficult it would be to repeat his '86 season. But despite the slow start, Clemens responded to the challenge.

COURTESY OF THE BOSTON RED SOX

He ended the year with four consecutive com-plete-game victories and finished the season with a 20–9 record, becoming the first consecutive 20-game winner in the American League since Tommy John accomplished the feat in 1979–80. Clemens led the American League in wins, shutouts (7), and complete games (18). He was named the American League's Cy Young Award winner for the second consecutive season. Only Koufax, McLain, and Jim Palmer had accomplished the unusual feat.

The 1988 and 1989 campaigns would have been outstanding years for any pitcher but Clemens. He finished 1988 with an 18–12 record, despite having an 0–5 record in August, and led the major leagues with 291 strikeouts. He won 17 games in 1989 and was second in the major leagues with 230 strikeouts.

In 1990, Clemens could have won his third Cy Young Award. Along with becoming the Red Sox's all-time strikeout leader, he won 21 games. His spar-kling 1.93 ERA was the best in the majors and the first under 2.00 in the American League since the Yankees' Ron Guidry finished with a 1.74 in 1978. But the Cy Young Award headed west to Oakland, where the A's Bob Welch won 27 games.

In game four of the 1990 American League play-offs against the A's, Clemens lost his temper follow-ing what he felt was a bad call by the home-plate umpire. Clemens cursed the umpire from the pitch-ing mound and, when he was ejected from the game, tried to grab the umpire. For his behavior, Clemens was fined $10,000 and given a five-game suspension for 1991.

Despite the suspension, which he served from April 26 to May 3, Clemens was at the top of his game in 1991. He won four games without a loss in April, and ran his record to 6–0 before losing a game. Despite a brief slump, his record was 11–5 at the All-Star break.

In September, he helped the Red Sox as they tried to catch the Toronto Blue Jays for the American League East title, posting a 4–0 record during the month. Only losses in his last two starts prevented him from winning 20 games for the fourth time in his career.

When the 1991 American League Cy Young winner was announced, Clemens was the easy choice. He finished the year with an 18–10 record and led the American League in strikeouts, shutouts, innings pitched, and ERA.

Despite losing his last three games in 1992, Clemens still finished the year with 18 wins. He led the American League in ERA (2.41) and shutouts (5) for the third consecutive year. The only other major league pitcher to accomplish this feat was Hall of Famer Grover Cleveland Alexander, from 1915 to 1917.

Clemens finished third in the 1992 American League Cy Young voting. Year after year, the Rocket continues to prove he is the best pitcher in the American League and, possibly, in all of baseball.

ROGER CLEMENS—CAREER STATISTICS

YEAR	CLUB	LEAGUE	G	IP	W	L	H	R	ER	SO	BB	ERA
1983	WINTER HAVEN	GULF COAST	4	29.0	3	1	22	4	4	36	0	1.24
	NEW BRITAIN	EASTERN	7	52.0	4	1	31	8	8	59	12	1.38
1984	PAWTUCKET	INTERNATIONAL	7	46.2	2	3	39	12	10	50	14	1.93
	BOSTON	AMERICAN	21	133.1	9	4	146	67	64	126	29	4.32
1985	BOSTON	AMERICAN	15	98.1	7	5	83	38	36	74	37	3.29
1986	BOSTON	AMERICAN	33	254.0	24	4	179	77	70	238	67	2.48
1987	BOSTON	AMERICAN	36	281.2	20	9	248	100	93	256	83	2.97
1988	BOSTON	AMERICAN	35	264.0	18	12	217	93	86	291	62	2.93
1989	BOSTON	AMERICAN	35	253.1	17	11	215	101	88	230	93	3.13
1990	BOSTON	AMERICAN	31	228.1	21	6	193	59	49	209	54	1.93
1991	BOSTON	AMERICAN	35	271.1	18	10	219	93	79	241	65	2.62
1992	BOSTON	AMERICAN	32	246.2	18	11	203	80	66	208	62	2.41
1993	BOSTON	AMERICAN	29	191.2	11	14	175	99	95	160	67	4.46
MAJOR LEAGUE TOTALS			**302**	**2222.2**	**163**	**86**	**1878**	**807**	**726**	**2033**	**619**	**2.94**

APPENDIX

CY YOUNG AWARD WINNERS

		W—L	SV	ERA
1956	*Don Newcombe, Bklyn (NL)	27—7	0	3.06
1957	Warren Spahn, Mil (NL)	21—11	3	2.69
1958	Bob Turley, NY (AL)	21—7	1	2.97
1959	Early Wynn, Chi (AL)	22—10	0	3.17
1960	Vernon Law, Pitt (NL)	20—9	0	3.08
1961	Whitey Ford, NY (AL)	25—4	0	3.21
1962	Don Drysdale, LA (NL)	25—9	1	2.83
1963	*Sandy Koufax, LA (NL)	25—5	0	1.88
1964	Dean Chance, LA (AL)	20—9	4	1.65
1965	Sandy Koufax, LA (NL)	26—8	2	2.04
1966	Sandy Koufax, LA (NL)	27—9	0	1.73
1967	Mike McCormick, SF (NL)	22—10	0	2.85
	Jim Lonborg, Bos (AL)	22—9	0	3.16
1968	*Bob Gibson, StL (NL)	22—9	0	1.12
	*Denny McLain, Det. (AL)	31—6	0	1.96
1969	Tom Seaver, NY (NL)	25—7	0	2.21
	Denny McLain, Det (AL)	24—9	0	2.80
	Mike Cuellar, Balt (AL)	23—11	0	2.38
1970	Bob Gibson, StL (NL)	23—7	0	3.12
	Jim Perry, Minn (AL)	24—12	0	3.03
1971	Ferguson Jenkins, Chi (NL)	24—13	0	2.77
	*Vida Blue, Oak (AL)	24—8	0	1.82

* Won MVP and Cy Young awards in same season.

		W—L	SV	ERA
1972	STEVE CARLTON, PHI (NL)	27—10	0	1.97
	GAYLORD PERRY, CLEV (AL)	24—16	1	1.92
1973	TOM SEAVER, NY (NL)	19—10	0	2.08
	JIM PALMER, BALT (AL)	22—9	1	2.40
1974	MIKE MARSHALL, LA (NL)	15—12	21	2.42
	CATFISH HUNTER, OAK (AL)	25—12	0	2.49
1975	TOM SEAVER, NY (NL)	22—9	0	2.38
	JIM PALMER, BALT. (AL)	23—11	1	2.09
1976	RANDY JONES, SD (NL)	22—14	0	2.74
	JIM PALMER, BALT. (AL)	22—13	0	2.51
1977	STEVE CARLTON, PHI (NL)	23—10	0	2.64
	SPARKY LYLE, NY (AL)	13—5	26	2.17
1978	GAYLORD PERRY, SD (NL)	21—6	0	2.72
	RON GUIDRY, NY (AL)	25—3	0	1.74
1979	BRUCE SUTTER, CHI (NL)	6—6	37	2.23
	MIKE FLANAGAN, BALT (AL)	23—9	0	3.08
1980	STEVE CARLTON, PHIL (NL)	24—9	0	2.34
	STEVE STONE, BALT (AL)	25—7	0	3.23
1981	F. VALENZUELA, LA (NL)	13—7	0	2.48
	*ROLLIE FINGERS, MIL (AL)	6—3	28	1.04
1982	STEVE CARLTON, PHIL (NL)	23—11	0	3.10
	PETE VUCKOVICH, MIL (AL)	18—6	0	3.34
1983	JOHN DENNY, PHIL (NL)	19—6	0	2.37
	LAMARR HOYT, CHI (AL)	24—10	0	3.66
1984	RICK SUTCLIFFE, CHI (NL)	16—1	0	2.69
	*WILLIE HERNANDEZ, DET (AL)	9—3	32	1.92
1985	DWIGHT GOODEN, NY (NL)	24—4	0	1.53
	BRET SABERHAGEN, KC (AL)	20—6	0	2.87
1986	MIKE SCOTT, HOU (NL)	18—10	0	2.22
	*ROGER CLEMENS, BOS (AL)	24—4	0	2.48

* WON MVP AND CY YOUNG AWARDS IN SAME SEASON.

		W—L	SV	ERA
1987	Steve Bedrosian, Phil (NL)	5—3	40	2.83
	Roger Clemens, Bos (AL)	20—9	0	2.97
1988	Orel Hershiser, LA (NL)	23—8	1	2.26
	Frank Viola, Minn (AL)	24—7	0	2.64
1989	Mark Davis, SD (NL)	4—3	44	1.85
	Bret Saberhagen, KC (AL)	23—6	0	2.16
1990	Doug Drabek, Pitt (NL)	22—6	0	2.76
	Bob Welch, Oak (AL)	27—6	0	2.95
1991	Tom Glavine, Atl (NY)	20—11	0	2.55
	Roger Clemens, Bos (AL)	18—10	0	2.62
1992	Greg Maddux, Chi (NL)	20—11	0	2.18
	Dennis Eckersley, Oak (AL)	7—1	51	1.91
1993	Greg Maddux, Atl (NL)	20—10	0	2.36
	Jack McDowell, Chi (AL)	22—10	0	3.37

INDEX